Stevie watched, dumbfounded, as Veronica pulled out a credit card and paid. "I can't believe it," she whispered to her friends. "She's buying *my* bridle! It's just not fair."

"She's just doing it to make you mad," Carole whispered back soothingly.

"Well, it's working," Stevie snapped. She glowered at Veronica, but the other girl didn't even glance at The Saddle Club as she took the bag from the clerk and sauntered out of the store.

"What a jerk," Lisa said when Veronica had gone. "Maybe we should be glad we're not rich like her, if that's what money does to your personality."

The salesclerk walked over to them. "Hello, girls," she said pleasantly. "I noticed you were looking at the bridle that young lady just bought. Are you interested in it? I have another one just like it in the back."

"No, thank you," Stevie said. "I'll just take this." She held up the cheek strap. "I don't have enough money for a whole new bridle."

But as the woman turned to lead her back to the cash register, Carole and Lisa heard Stevie mutter under her breath, "Not yet, anyway."

THE SADDLE CLUB

HORSE-SITTERS

BONNIE BRYANT

A SKYLARK BOOK
NEW YORK • TORONTO • LONDON • SYDNEY • AUCKLAND

*I would like to express my special thanks
to Catherine Hapka for her
help in the writing of this book.*

RL 5, 009–012

HORSE-SITTERS
A Skylark Book / April 1996

ISBN 0-553-48363-3

Published simultaneously in the United States and Canada

PRINTED IN THE UNITED STATES OF AMERICA
OPM   0 9 8 7 6 5 4 3 2 1

"OKAY. I'M FINISHED," Stevie Lake said, licking the last few drops of tomato sauce off her fingers. "Let's go. I want to get to The Saddlery before it closes."

Stevie—short for Stephanie—and her two best friends, Carole Hanson and Lisa Atwood, were at the mall near their hometown of Willow Creek, Virginia. They had just finished a post-riding-lesson snack at the pizza parlor.

"Don't worry, we have plenty of time. It's too bad about your bridle," Lisa told Stevie sympathetically, pulling her wallet out of her backpack. "You haven't had it very long."

That day in riding class one of the cheek straps on Stevie's bridle had snapped in two. She was planning to buy a new cheek strap at The Saddlery, the tack shop at the mall. "I know. But

1

I'm not surprised. I bought it secondhand, and it was pretty well worn when I got it." Stevie shrugged. "But it was the best I could afford."

Carole peered into her change purse glumly. "Speaking of affording things, I hope I can afford that pizza I just ate," she commented, pouring a small pile of pennies onto the table. "I'm practically broke. Thanks to the library fines for that book I just found under my bed, I'm already borrowing against next week's allowance."

Lisa giggled. "I still can't believe you lost a book under your bed for six months." Lisa was very neat and organized, and it was sometimes hard for her to understand how disorganized Stevie and Carole could be. Stevie cared much more about having fun than about being organized and responsible. She was so messy and chaotic that her parents had long ago declared her bedroom a national disaster area. Carole could also be disorganized, but in a different way. She could be flaky, and she tended to forget what she was doing—except at the stable. There, Carole was anything but scatterbrained.

But Lisa knew that their different personalities were part of what made the three of them friends. In fact, they were such good friends that they had formed The Saddle Club. It had only two rules: Members had to be horse-crazy, and they had to be willing to help one another out. The first part was no problem, since all three girls loved riding together at Pine Hollow Stables. Their riding instructor and the owner of Pine Hollow, Max Regnery, liked to say that The Saddle Club spent more time at

2

the stable than he did. The second part was usually easy, too—although in the case of overdue library books there was little that even the best of friends could do other than sympathize.

"Chad once lost two library books under his bed for a whole year," Stevie commented. Chad was the oldest of her three brothers. "He had to get a newspaper route just to pay the fines."

Lisa put some money on the table. "I can lend you a dollar if you need it, Carole," she offered. "That's all I have left. I spent all my extra cash on a subscription to that photography magazine."

"At least I'm not the only one who's broke this time," Stevie said as Lisa counted the money on the table to make sure it was enough. Stevie's parents paid her a weekly allowance, but it usually took her much less than a week to spend it.

"Do you have enough to buy a new cheek strap?" Carole asked.

"Barely," Stevie replied. She sighed. "I wish I could buy Belle a whole new bridle. That old one is so ratty-looking. My horse deserves better."

"Sure she does," Carole said. "But bridles are expensive, and Belle doesn't care what her tack looks like as long as it's clean and in good working condition."

"But *I* care," Stevie said. "Belle is so beautiful. A new bridle would make her look even better."

Lisa raised an eyebrow. "Really?" she teased. "Is this my friend Stevie Lake, fashion plate, talking?"

Stevie glanced down at her wrinkled T-shirt and patched, faded jeans and grinned. "Hey, I may not be much of a fashion plate, but Belle could be if she had half a chance."

"I know what you mean, Stevie," said Carole as the three friends left the restaurant and strolled toward the Saddlery, which was located at the other end of the mall. "But the truth is, there are more important things than how a horse looks. And Belle is all those things. Look how well she did today."

"She did do well, didn't she?" Stevie said proudly. That day in their riding class, they had begun teaching their horses to do a trotting half-pass, a dressage movement in which a horse moves diagonally, spine straight and head bent in the direction it's going. All the horses could perform the move at a walk, but it was a new challenge to learn it at a trot. Belle was the only horse that had performed the trotting half-pass almost perfectly.

"I'm sure it didn't hurt that you and Belle have been practicing that move outside of class for the last month," Lisa teased, dodging a stroller pushed by a distracted shopper.

"Did you notice who else was doing well?" Carole commented.

"You mean Veronica and Danny?" Lisa said, wrinkling her nose in distaste. Veronica diAngelo was a better-than-average rider, and her horse, Danny, was gorgeous, well bred, and perfectly trained. But that didn't mean The Saddle Club liked her. The spoiled rich girl was snobby and sneaky, and she liked nothing better than making herself look good at someone else's expense.

"They did pretty well, too," Carole said grudgingly. "But that

wasn't who I meant. I was talking about Polly and Romeo."
Polly Giacomin was another member of their class. She owned
her own horse, a lively chocolate-brown gelding named Romeo.
Romeo was making excellent progress in dressage. He was smart
and eager, and Polly had been working hard on his training.

"I noticed that, too," Stevie said. "Romeo's pretty talented."
She kicked at an empty paper cup that someone had dropped on
the mall floor. "Besides, Polly's parents bought her all that beautiful new tack when she got him. He could hardly help doing
well in that."

Carole and Lisa exchanged glances. They both knew that a
horse couldn't care less what its tack looked like. They also
knew that Stevie knew that, and that she was just feeling
grumpy because she couldn't afford a new bridle for Belle.

Carole decided it was time to change the subject. "Isn't Deborah's aunt coming to visit soon?" she asked, stooping to retrieve
the paper cup and dumping it in a nearby trash can. Deborah
was Max's wife. She was an investigative reporter for a newspaper in nearby Washington, D.C.

"It's her great-aunt," Lisa corrected. "Her name is Eugenia.
Doesn't that sound old-fashioned? She's arriving on Thursday.
When I was in the tack room today I overheard Deborah talking
to Mrs. Reg about picking her up."

"From the airport?" Stevie asked.

"No," Lisa said, pausing for a second to glance in the window
of the bookstore. "They were talking about driving to get her in
one of Max's horse trailers. I guess she lives a couple of hours
away, and she's bringing her own horse with her."

"Really?" Carole said, suddenly looking more interested. Someone who would bring a horse along on a family visit sounded like someone she'd like to meet. "What kind of horse?"

"I don't know, Carole," Lisa said with a laugh. "I told you, I just overheard part of the conversation."

"Well, I guess we'll find out soon enough," Carole said. "I can't wait to meet her."

"Max doesn't seem to be looking forward to her visit, though, does he?" Stevie commented. "Every time Deborah mentions her great-aunt, he starts stammering and looking nervous in that weird way he has. Did you notice?"

"You're right," Lisa said thoughtfully. "I hadn't really thought about it, but I did notice it. I wonder what that's all about."

Carole shrugged. "I have no idea," she said. "It's not as if he's meeting her for the first time—he and Deborah went to visit her right after their wedding. And after all, how bad could a fellow horseperson be?"

"I have two words for you in answer to that," Stevie said, raising her voice to be heard above a gaggle of small children who were rushing by toward the toy store. "Veronica diAngelo."

Carole rolled her eyes. "She certainly has been annoying lately, hasn't she?" she said. "After Danny's great performance in class today you'd think Veronica would at least give him a pat or something. But instead she just tossed the reins to Red the second she dismounted." Red O'Malley was Pine Hollow's head stable hand. Even though riders were supposed to do their share of the stable chores, including taking care of the horses they rode, Veronica usually treated Red as her personal servant.

6

The girls had reached The Saddlery. As soon as they entered, Stevie headed for the section of the store that held bins and baskets of small tack pieces. Carole and Lisa stood by the entrance for a moment, looking around and breathing in the rich leathery smell.

"I'm going to check out the clothing rack," Lisa decided. "I want to see if they still have those schooling chaps I tried on last month."

Carole nodded. She remembered the beautiful soft leather chaps. They had fit Lisa perfectly. They were expensive, though —if Lisa saved her allowance for months she still couldn't afford them. But Carole knew her friend couldn't resist looking at them every time she was in the store.

"I guess I'll just browse," Carole said, wandering toward a shelf full of books and videos near the cash register. She flipped through several of the books. She liked reading anything she could get her hands on about horses and riding, and her room at home held a small library of books and magazines she had bought or received as gifts. But more often she just borrowed books from the Willow Creek Public Library. It was usually cheaper that way—unless, of course, she happened to misplace one of the books under her bed.

A large red box caught her eye. It was a set of videos called *The Complete Horse*. Carole picked it up and read the back of the box.

"What are you looking at?" Lisa asked from behind her.

Carole jumped, startled. "Oh! It's this," she said, handing the box to Lisa.

7

Lisa scanned the description of the contents. "Wow," she said, and read aloud: " 'This nine-video set is the answer to every serious horseman's prayers. Volume one, the breeds . . .' It sounds like they cover every breed of horse known to man." She read a little more, then said, "The rest of the tapes sound just as interesting. Here's one on show training and dressage, one on equine medicine, another on the history of the horse, another on everything you need to know to run your own sta—"

"I have to have it," Carole interrupted excitedly. "It sounds great."

Lisa flipped over the box and glanced at the price tag. "Wow," she said again. "All this knowledge doesn't come cheap."

Carole looked at the tag, too. Her face fell. "Oh well," she said quietly. She didn't even bother to calculate how long it would take her to save the necessary amount. "Maybe my dad will buy it for me for Christmas."

"I was just thinking the same thing about those chaps," Lisa said sadly. "The worst part is, they're actually on sale right now. But they're still more than I can afford."

"Come on," Carole said, carefully sliding *The Complete Horse* back onto the shelf. "Let's go see how Stevie's doing."

They found her at the other end of the store in front of a rack full of brand-new bridles. "Any luck, Stevie?" Carole asked.

Stevie nodded and held up a new cheek strap. But her eyes were trained on one of the bridles in front of her. "Would you look at that?" she said, gesturing at it. "Wouldn't that look perfect on Belle?"

8

Her friends had to agree that it would. The bridle was made of buttery-soft leather. The noseband was stitched and the reins were braided.

"It's beautiful," Lisa said sincerely.

Stevie reached up and carefully took down the bridle. She read the price tag and frowned. "It's not fair," she complained. "Why does it have to cost so much?"

Before her friends could answer, they all heard the tinkling of the bell above the door, and then a familiar commanding voice.

"Excuse me. You there. Do you have any brown bootlaces?" Veronica demanded of the salesclerk.

The woman stepped forward. "Of course, miss," she said. "They're right over here. What length do you need?"

Veronica ignored the clerk's question. She had just noticed The Saddle Club. "Well, well, well," she said, strolling over to them. "If it isn't show-off Stevie and her little fan club. You thought you were pretty clever in class today, didn't you? But I know the truth. I saw you practicing that trotting half-pass last week."

"So what?" Stevie asked, annoyed.

"So I'm going to tell Max," Veronica replied. "I know you're just trying to show up the rest of us, and he should know it, too."

Carole and Lisa tried to stifle their giggles. Veronica was really stretching to pick a fight this time. First of all, Max already knew that Stevie and Belle had been practicing. It was obvious. No horse could do a trotting half-pass that well on the first try. Second, there was no reason at all Max would mind a student practicing her skills outside of class. Obviously that idea was foreign to Veronica.

"If you spent less time shopping and more time riding, maybe you and Danny could be *almost* as good as Belle and I are," Stevie retorted. "Then again, probably not." She turned her back on Veronica and hung the bridle back on its hook.

"What's that?" Veronica asked. She snatched the bridle down again and turned it over in her hands. "Hmm, this is nice. I'm surprised you would even bother to look at it, Stevie. It's much too expensive for you."

"Don't be so sure," Stevie said. "You're not the only one who can buy nice things, you know. And this bridle will look great on Belle."

"You may be right," Veronica said sweetly. "Does that mean you're buying it for her? After all, you saw it first." She waited a moment. Stevie was silent. "Oh, good. I'll take that as a no. Because the truth is, this bridle will look fabulous on Danny." She marched over to the counter, where the salesclerk was waiting with the bootlaces. "I'll take this, too," she said loudly, laying the bridle on the counter.

Stevie watched, dumbfounded, as Veronica pulled out a credit card and paid. "I can't believe it," she whispered to her friends. "She's buying *my* bridle! It's just not fair."

"She's just doing it to make you mad," Carole whispered back soothingly.

"Well, it's working," Stevie snapped. She glowered at Veronica, but the other girl didn't even glance at The Saddle Club as she took the bag from the clerk and sauntered out of the store.

"What a jerk," Lisa said when Veronica had gone. "Maybe we should be glad we're not rich like her, if that's what money does to your personality."

The salesclerk walked over to them. "Hello, girls," she said pleasantly. "I noticed you were looking at the bridle that young lady just bought. Are you interested in it? I have another one just like it in the back."

"No, thank you," Stevie said. "I'll just take this." She held up the cheek strap. "I don't have enough money for a whole new bridle."

But as the woman turned to lead her back to the cash register, Carole and Lisa heard Stevie mutter under her breath, "Not yet, anyway."

CAROLE RELUCTANTLY PULLED her feet out of the cool water of Willow Creek. "I guess we should head back now," she said. It was the warmest day of spring so far, and the girls had headed for Pine Hollow right after school for a trail ride. They had ended up at their favorite spot, a secluded area along the banks of the creek that had given their town its name. Their horses were dozing in the shade nearby as the girls dunked their feet in the running water.

"Do we have to?" Stevie moaned. She was lying on her back, eyes closed, legs dangling off the bank. "It's so nice here."

Lisa stood up and stretched, then reached for her socks and boots. "Don't worry, Stevie. We'll have all summer to do this," she reminded her.

"If I survive that long," Stevie said, opening her eyes but not sitting up. "I can't believe how much work my teachers have been giving out lately. Haven't they ever heard of winding down the school year?"

Carole laughed. "If you had your way, the school year would start winding down around the second week in September."

"No, the first week," Stevie corrected with a grin. She sat up and reached for her socks. "Anyway, I guess we should be getting back. I just remembered—Aunt Eugenia will be here soon."

"How could you forget?" Lisa asked, rolling her eyes. "Max has been running around frantically for the last day and a half."

"I don't understand it," Carole said, perching on a rock while she waited for her friends to finish putting on their boots. "Max is usually so levelheaded about everything. The last time I saw him this distracted was when he had just met Deborah."

"Maybe he's in love with Aunt Eugenia," Stevie joked.

Lisa shook her head thoughtfully. "I doubt it," she said, "but there is something going on. I wonder what?"

"Max is probably just in a weird mood or something," Stevie said with a shrug. "Anyway, we have more important things to think about, remember?"

Carole groaned. "Please, Stevie. Don't start up about your moneymaking schemes again. That's all you've been able to talk about since Veronica bought that stupid bridle the other day."

Stevie looked hurt. "What do you mean?" she protested. "This isn't just about the bridle—although Belle does deserve it. I'm also trying to think of ways to raise money for your stuff." Carole and Lisa had pointed out how much they wanted the

13

videos and the chaps. They'd been trying to make her feel better about not being able to afford a new bridle, but the plan had backfired. Stevie was determined that The Saddle Club should have all the things they wanted, and she had been coming up with all sorts of wild schemes to earn money.

"Come on, Stevie," Lisa said. "Most of your plans have been pretty, well, *impractical*."

"No they haven't," Stevie said. "I still think we could raise a lot of money by holding a bake sale outside the supermarket. My brother's scout troop did it, and they made a nice profit."

"Your brother's scout troop had two dozen parents baking for them," Carole reminded her. "Besides, I'm not sure most people would think donating money for Lisa's new riding chaps is quite as worthy a cause."

"Well, how about my party-planning service?" Stevie said. "The Saddle Club knows how to plan a great party. We've done it plenty of times for free. Why shouldn't we get paid for it?"

"Nobody wants to spend a lot of money to hire someone to plan their party unless it's a wedding or something," Lisa said. "And nobody's going to hire people our age to plan their wedding."

"My personal favorite was your plan to get Max to pay us to repave the driveway and parking area at Pine Hollow," Carole said with a laugh as she walked over to her bay gelding, Starlight, and got ready to mount.

"How about the one where she had the three of us mowing every field and lawn in the county with Max's little riding mower?" Lisa added.

14

"Of course, he'd probably demand a share of our profits for the use of the mower," Carole pointed out. "That's why I prefer the one where she has *you* giving ballet lessons to little kids in *my* basement. No overhead, you know."

By this time Carole and Lisa were both laughing, but Stevie didn't look nearly as amused. "Very funny," she said huffily, swinging up onto Belle's back. "Here I am trying to help you out, and you're treating it like a big joke." She urged Belle into a trot and headed off down the trail.

Carole glanced at Lisa and shrugged. Stevie had a quick temper, but she usually didn't stay angry for long. Besides, her friends knew it was really Veronica that Stevie was mad at, not them.

"I guess this isn't the best time to mention my other favorite Stevie plan," Carole said.

"You mean the one where she sells off her brothers to the highest bidder?" Lisa guessed.

Carole grinned. "Exactly."

A SHORT WHILE later The Saddle Club arrived back at Pine Hollow. Carole and Lisa had caught up to Stevie moments after leaving the spot by the creek. As they'd expected, she had already forgotten all about her annoyance and was busy thinking up new moneymaking ideas.

As the girls dismounted and started to lead their horses inside, Stevie was chattering about her latest brainstorm, which involved franchising lemonade stands to all the elementary-school kids in the area. But Carole's attention was drawn to

-another conversation taking place nearby. Polly Giacomin was standing near the outdoor ring talking to Max. She seemed worried, but Max wasn't paying much attention to her. Instead he kept glancing at his watch and then at the driveway. Carole guessed that he was waiting for Eugenia's arrival, but she couldn't believe he was so distracted that he wasn't even listening to Polly. Carole slowed down, trying to hear what was going on. Her friends noticed and did the same. Even Stevie stopped talking.

"But, Max," Polly was saying urgently, "do you think he'll forget everything he's learned while I'm away? I'll be gone for almost a week, and this dressage stuff is still pretty new to him."

"Mmm," was Max's only reply. "When did you say you're leaving, Meg? Um—I mean, Polly?"

"Tomorrow morning," Polly said, looking annoyed. The Saddle Club guessed that it wasn't the first—or even the second—time she had said it. "I won't be back until next Wednesday night. What do you think we should do?"

"Do?" Max repeated, glancing at his watch again. "What do you mean, Veron—er, Polly?"

The Saddle Club could see Polly taking a deep breath. "What should we do about Romeo's dressage training? I hate to think he'll forget everything while I'm gone if nobody works with him."

"Don't worry, Polly," Max said, peering over her head toward the road at the end of the drive. "Red will see that Danny—er, Starlight—er, I mean, Romeo will get some exercise while you're away. Don't worry about a thing."

16

Polly rolled her eyes. "Thanks, Max," she said sarcastically, turning and stomping away.

Max didn't even notice. He glanced at his watch again, then spun on his heel and headed inside.

The Saddle Club exchanged mystified glances. It wasn't at all like Max to ignore a rider's concerns, especially since Polly was right. Romeo had been making wonderful progress lately in his dressage training, but if nobody worked with the horse for almost a week, it was quite possible he would backslide. Carole spoke up and said so.

"I know," Lisa said. "It would be a shame if all Polly's hard work went to waste just because Max is acting bizarre for some reason. What do you think could be the matter with him?"

Carole shrugged in response, but Stevie didn't seem to have heard the question. She was staring in the direction Max and Polly had gone with a thoughtful look on her face.

"Stevie?" Lisa said. "What is it?"

"Hmm?" Stevie said. "Oh, nothing. Come on, let's get the horses settled. Aunt Eugenia should be here soon, and I don't want to miss meeting the woman who has that kind of effect on Max."

THE GIRLS FINISHED their stable chores just in time to see Max's small horse van trundle slowly up the driveway with Deborah at the wheel. She brought the vehicle to a careful stop, then opened the door and jumped out. She paused long enough to give Max a peck on the cheek and the girls a cheerful wave.

Then she walked around to the passenger side and opened the door.

"It's about time, Deborah," a strident, high-pitched voice said from inside the cab. "I thought you were planning to leave me sitting in here all evening."

Deborah laughed. "Don't be silly, Aunt Genie," she replied. She held out her arm to help the owner of the voice climb out of the trailer. The woman who emerged was white-haired and wrinkled, but despite her obvious age she appeared hearty and energetic. Carole wondered why she hadn't simply opened the door and climbed out herself.

Max stepped forward. "Hello, Aunt Eugenia," he said in a quiet, tentative voice. "I hope you had a pleasant trip."

The old woman stared at him coldly. "Hardly," she said, drawing out the single word until it sounded like a whole sentence. "Deborah drove like a maniac. I've never been so terrified in my life. And my poor baby Honeybee must be beside herself. She's not used to such treatment."

Deborah smiled and shook her head. "Really, Aunt Genie," she said. "The way you go on!" She turned to Max. "I don't think we hit forty miles per hour the whole way here."

"Hmmph," Eugenia replied. She peered past Max at the three girls, who were watching in silence. "And whom have we here?" she inquired suspiciously.

"These are three of Max's best young riders," Deborah replied, waving The Saddle Club over. She introduced them each by name. Lisa, well trained by her mother, stepped forward to offer the old woman her hand.

18

"How do you do, Ms. Eugenia," she said politely.

Eugenia took Lisa's hand limply and stared intently into her eyes. "Are my old ears failing me at last? This seems to be a young lady with some manners." She dropped Lisa's hand and turned back to Max. "I thought all young people these days were like you and my Deborah, here—unschooled and boorish."

Stevie glanced at Max eagerly, waiting for his response. She was sure he'd be annoyed by the insult and say so. But she was disappointed.

"Would you like to come up to the house, Aunt Eugenia?" Max said, smiling blandly. "I'm sure you could use some re-freshment after your trip. My mother has some tea ready for you."

"Are you mad, young man?" Eugenia snapped. "What about my poor baby, trapped back there in that cramped little vehicle you call a horse trailer?" She snorted. "Horse trailer, indeed. Barely enough room for a good-sized cat back there." She stomped around to the back of the van with Max and Deborah right behind her. The Saddle Club followed, not wanting to miss a thing.

Stevie was doing her best not to break into a grin. Someone was scolding Max—the man who scolded them for a living!

"Of course, Aunt Eugenia," Max said quickly. "I was going to have Red settle her in for you. You don't have to worry."

"Oh, don't I?" Eugenia said sharply. "I'll be the judge of that, if you don't mind." She started to pull at the heavy pin holding the van doors shut.

Deborah stepped forward and gently pushed Eugenia's hands

aside. "Don't be silly, dear," she scolded. "The door is much too heavy for you."

"Let me do it," Stevie offered quickly, stepping forward.

Eugenia peered at her. "Is this how you run things here, Max?" she said testily. "Having young girls do all the work while you sit around and collect the money?"

The statement was so outrageous that Carole was sure Max would have to respond. But although she thought she saw his meek smile falter for a split second, he didn't say a word.

"Don't be silly, Aunt Genie," Deborah teased good-naturedly. "I've told you how hard Max works. Why, I hardly get to see him as it is. If you put ideas into his head, he may never have any time for me at all, and then where would I be?"

"You might be better off, for all I know," Eugenia replied shortly. "But more importantly, if he's so terminally overworked, I suppose I'll have to take care of my Honeybee myself, hmm?"

"Of course not, Aunt Eugenia," Max put in. "She'll have top-notch care here during your visit, just like all my horses."

"My horse is not just like all your horses, young man," Eugenia said. "She requires special care. Her veterinarian has her on several different medications, and it's very important that she receive proper attention. Someone needs to monitor her closely."

"I understand your concerns, Aunt Eugenia," Max said carefully. "But the truth is, Red and I do monitor all our horses with the greatest care. So there's really no need for you to worry."

Eugenia drew herself up to her full height. "I see," she said coldly. "If I understand what you're telling me, I can't expect my

Honeybee to receive any special treatment while she's here. I suppose that means I'll have to hire someone myself to come in and give her the care she needs."

Max opened his mouth to answer, but before he could say a word Stevie broke in. "I have just the solution, Ms. Eugenia," she said quickly. "May I offer you the services of my friends and myself—experienced horse-sitters!"

A FEW MOMENTS later the deal was final. Carole and Lisa, stunned, watched as Eugenia and Deborah, arm in arm, headed off toward the house with Max trailing rather forlornly behind them.

As soon as the adults were out of sight, Carole turned to Stevie. "Are you crazy?" she asked.

"Like a fox," Stevie declared proudly. "Didn't you hear how much she's going to pay us? And all we have to do is take care of one horse for a few days. This is the best moneymaking idea ever. And it fell right into our laps."

Lisa shrugged. "I guess it could be okay," she said. "It's not going to pay for your new bridle—let alone the other stuff—but it's a good bit of money. And even with school and riding lessons and everything else, it shouldn't take up too much time if we all work together."

"Right," Stevie agreed. "Now, come on, let's get Honeybee put away. Max said we should put her in that empty stall next to Nero's. It's all ready for her. We want to make sure the old girl is settled in before Aunt Genie finishes her tea." With that, she swung open the doors of the trailer, revealing a wide palomino rump. At that moment, a loud snort came from somewhere beyond that rump, and then an even louder whinny.

"Uh-oh, not a moment too soon," Carole said. "It sounds like Honeybee wants out." While Stevie set up the ramp, Carole climbed into the trailer and went to the horse's head, talking soothingly all the while. But as soon as she reached for the old mare's halter, Honeybee's head darted forward, and she bared her teeth. Carole just avoided getting her hand nipped.

She continued talking softly to the mare. After a moment she tried again, with the same result.

"What's going on in there?" Stevie asked, poking her head in.

"I don't think Honeybee likes me," Carole said. "Either that, or she's happier being in this trailer than we thought. She won't let me touch her halter."

"Let me try," Stevie offered.

Carole gladly traded places with her. She climbed out of the van and told Lisa what was going on.

"I hope that doesn't mean Aunt Eugenia's personality has rubbed off on her horse," Lisa said.

Carole shook her head. "She really is something, isn't she?" she said. "I can't believe Max let her get away with all those

23

things she was saying about him. He's so proud of Pine Hollow —with good reason—and she was practically insulting it right to his face."

"Not to mention insulting *him*," Lisa added. She glanced up at the van. "Look, Stevie's got her going."

Sure enough, Honeybee's wide hindquarters were moving slowly backward as Stevie guided the mare down the ramp. "Great," Carole said. "I guess Stevie doesn't taste as good as I do."

"Don't be so sure about that," Lisa said with a grin.

Carole looked again and saw that Honeybee's ears were pinned back and she had a large chunk of Stevie's long hair in her mouth. She seemed to be rolling it around between her teeth. Stevie's own teeth were gritted, but she was speaking patiently to the horse as she led her out of the van. "I had to trick her," she told her friends, speaking in the same soothing voice so that Honeybee would think she was still talking to her. "I was trying to distract her by waving my left hand at one side of her head while I grabbed the halter with my right hand. But she was more distracted by my hair."

Finally Honeybee was safely on the ground. Lisa stepped forward to take hold of the mare's halter, and as Honeybee turned to try to nip at her, Stevie managed to yank most of her hair free —although a few dark-blond strands still trailed from the horse's rubbery lips.

"Boy, she's a quick one, isn't she?" Lisa commented, barely managing to avoid the big teeth. Luckily the mare seemed to lose interest in trying to nip. Instead she swung her head around, nearly yanking Lisa's arm out of its socket as she took in the scene around her.

"Who knew such an old horse would have so much energy?" Stevie said, rubbing her head gingerly where the hairs had been yanked out.

"Are you all right, Lisa?" Carole asked.

Lisa nodded quickly as she tried to follow Honeybee's moves. The old mare wasn't very tall—probably about fifteen hands by Carole's guess—but she was fat, and she seemed to be strong, judging by the way she was dragging Lisa around.

Carole hurried forward and reached for the other side of the halter. Honeybee tried to nip her again, but only halfheartedly. She seemed too distracted by her new surroundings to pay much attention.

"Come on," Carole said, once she had a good grip on the halter. "Let's take her inside before she gets any more worked up."

Stevie hurried ahead to open the door. Carole and Lisa led the mare toward the stable building, but their progress was slow, since Honeybee seemed determined to smell and taste everything she passed. First she stopped to nibble at a fence post; then she tried to lower her head to sample a patch of grass beside the path. Then there was the stable doorway itself, which the horse chewed on for several seconds before Carole and Lisa managed to yank her head away.

Finally the girls got Honeybee moving toward her temporary

stall. Several horses peered out as the mare clattered past, including Polly Giacomin's horse, Romeo. Nero, the oldest horse in the stable, put his head out over his half door to see who was coming. He reached out to snuffle curiously at the newcomer, but his reward was a sharp nip on the nose. He threw up his head in dismay and backed away, disappearing into his stall.

"Sorry about that, Nero, old boy," Carole called to him breathlessly. "I guess Honeybee doesn't like other horses any more than she likes people."

Stevie opened the door to the empty stall next to Nero's. Honeybee was reluctant to go inside at first, but when Lisa grabbed some hay from the feed bin, which Red had filled, the mare followed her eagerly inside.

"Whew!" Lisa exclaimed. "Who was saying this job would be easy?"

"It's not over yet," Carole reminded her. "We really should groom her after her trip. And we definitely need to take off her traveling bandages. And once Aunt Eugenia comes back we'll have to get the details about the medicines she was talking about."

"Right," Stevie said. "They're probably in the van. Her grooming stuff might be there, too—I bet Aunt Genie brought along Honeybee's own brushes and rags. Only the best for her baby, you know."

"You're probably right," Carole said. "Will you run out and check while Lisa and I get started here?"

But Stevie's attention had just been caught by something

farther down the stable aisle. "Um, would you mind doing it? There's something important I have to take care of first."

Carole and Lisa exchanged glances and shrugged. "I'll go," Lisa offered.

"Good," Stevie said, hurrying off with a little wave.

"What do you think she's up to now?" Lisa asked Carole.

"I have no idea," Carole said. "But we don't have time to worry about it right now. Not if we're going to be successful horse-sitters, that is. I'll go put Honeybee on cross ties while you get her stuff. I think it will take both of us to groom her." With that, the two girls hurried off in opposite directions.

It wasn't easy, but the two girls managed to get Honeybee groomed and settled. The old mare nipped at every brush and rag they used, and often at the fingers holding them, but thanks to the girls' quickness they managed to escape without injury. They had just closed and latched the stall door when Stevie reappeared.

"Where have you been?" Carole asked, a little annoyed that Stevie had managed to miss all the work.

"Oh, are you finished already?" Stevie asked, glancing over the half door at the old mare. Honeybee was munching contentedly on a mouthful of hay. "Sorry about that. I didn't think my errand would take so long."

"You can stop being so mysterious already, Stevie," Lisa said, just as annoyed as Carole. The way she figured it, the only way The Saddle Club would be able to handle the responsibility they had taken on was if they all worked together. And that meant no running off when there was work to be done, no matter what the errand. "Where were you?"

Stevie broke into a cat-that-ate-the-canary grin. "I was in the locker room negotiating the deal for our second client," she announced.

"Our second client?" Carole repeated blankly. "What do you mean?"

"I mean the Saddle Club Horse-Sitting Service is really in business now," Stevie said. "We're going to take care of Romeo while Polly is out of town."

It took a moment for that to sink in. But when it did, Lisa and Carole spoke up in one voice. "Are you crazy?" they exclaimed.

"Stop asking me that," Stevie said, frowning. "Don't you see? The more clients we take on, the more money we earn toward the stuff we want at The Saddlery. Polly just called her parents, and they were happy to pay us the same fee we're getting from Aunt Eugenia. All we have to do is help out with Romeo's usual care and, more importantly, see that he keeps up with his dressage lessons until Polly comes back." She smiled. "Polly was so impressed with how well Belle and I did in class the other day that she's sure Romeo will be in good hands."

"I don't know, Stevie," Lisa said doubtfully. "We were already worried about fitting in Honeybee's care. And now we're supposed to take care of another horse?"

Stevie waved one hand. "*You* were worried," she corrected.

"But I'm not. Sure, Honeybee is a handful, but taking care of Romeo will be a breeze. Red will handle his morning feeding. All we have to do is exercise him and settle him in for the night."

"And go to school, do homework, go to riding class, take care of our regular stable chores . . . ," Lisa recited, ticking off each item on her fingers.

"Don't be such a worrywart," Stevie said. "It's just for a few days. And think of all the money we'll be making. It still won't be anywhere near enough to pay for everything, but at least it's a good start."

Carole looked thoughtful. "You may be right, Stevie," she admitted. "We'll have to put in a little extra time here at Pine Hollow, but with some careful planning it should be okay."

Lisa shrugged and sighed. "Well, maybe you're right," she said. "I guess two horses won't be that much trouble."

"That's the spirit," Stevie said. "Now come on, let's go out and wait for Aunt Genie. We'll ask her about that medicine and then we'll be done."

"Good," Carole said, rubbing her stomach. "It's almost dinnertime, and I'm starving. Wrestling with Honeybee really gave me an appetite."

The Saddle Club strolled down the aisle. As they turned the corner toward the entrance, they nearly collided with a breathless Veronica diAngelo, who was hurrying along at breakneck speed.

"Watch where you're going," she snapped.

"Same to you," Stevie retorted. "You know Max's rules about running in the stable."

Veronica ignored her comment. "Where's Max?" she demanded. "I need to speak to him immediately."

"He's not here," Lisa replied. She *could* have told Veronica that Max was just up at the house and that he would be returning soon, but somehow she didn't feel like sharing that information.

"What do you mean, he's not here?" Veronica said in annoyance.

"She means that this place, the place where you are right now, is exactly where Max *isn't* right now," Stevie replied. "Which part didn't you understand?"

"Shut up, Stevie," Veronica said. "I need to see Max. It's very important."

"Is something wrong with Danny?" Carole asked with concern. As much as she disliked Veronica, she would never want a horse to be in danger.

"Of course not. He's perfect as always," Veronica replied haughtily. "The matter I have to discuss with Max is private. In other words, none of your business." She tossed back her long, black hair. "One thing I can tell you, though. If Max knows what's good for him, he'll have to start spending a little more time around the stable for the next week or so." With that, she turned and stomped away.

"I wonder what that was all about," Lisa said.

"I don't," Stevie said. "She probably broke a nail cleaning tack and wants to tell Max she's suing him."

"Don't be ridiculous, Stevie," Carole replied. "What would Veronica be doing cleaning tack?" All three girls laughed.

"Come to think of it, what's Veronica doing here today at all?" Lisa said after a moment. "We didn't have a riding lesson today, and she certainly didn't show up to put in a few hours' work mucking out stalls."

Before her friends could reply, the girls heard another voice calling their names. They turned to see Mr. French, one of Max's adult riders, approaching.

Carole smiled at him. "Hi, Mr. French," she said. The other girls added their greetings. They all liked the friendly man. He worked for the State Department in Washington, D.C., which meant he always had plenty of interesting stories to tell. More importantly, he was an enthusiastic rider, even though he hadn't been doing it for very long. Recently Mr. French had bought his own horse, a Tennessee walking horse named Memphis. The mare was a beautiful chestnut with smooth gaits and a gentle, even disposition.

"Hi, girls," Mr. French said. "I'm glad I caught you. Listen, I was just talking to a friend of yours in the tack room—Polly Giacomin. She tells me you'll be keeping up with her horse's training while she's out of town."

"That's right," Stevie said proudly. "We've just started a new career as professional horse-sitters. Training, grooming, exercising—we do it all."

"I'm glad to hear it," Mr. French said with a smile. "Actually, I was hoping to engage your professional services myself. I just found out I have to leave the country for a week, and I was hoping you'd look after Memphis for me while I'm gone. Of course I'd pay you the going rate."

Lisa spoke up before Stevie could open her mouth. "It was very nice of you to think of us, Mr. French," she said politely. "And we'd love to take care of your beautiful horse for you. But really, there's no need to pay us to do what Max will gladly do for free. Well, for your usual boarding fees, that is."

"I know," Mr. French said. "But Max seems a little distracted these days. And you may have noticed I've been schooling Memphis on her running walk."

"I saw you practicing the other day," Carole said eagerly. The running walk was a distinctive gait found only in the Tennessee walking horse. It was a very fast, gliding walk accompanied by a rhythmic nodding of the head. "The running walk is an inherited gait," Carole explained to Lisa and Stevie. "You can't teach horses to do it, but you can sometimes work with them to improve it." She turned back to Mr. French. "Memphis seems to be responding well."

"Then you can understand why I'd rather pay a little extra to have someone do a little extra. I know Max and Red will give her perfect care—feed her, keep her stall clean, and so on—but they probably won't have time to ride or school her." He smiled at Carole. "And since I gather from your comments that you know something about what I've been doing, I'm more certain than ever that you girls are the best ones for the job. So what do you say?"

"We say we'd love to," Stevie said quickly, before Carole or

Lisa could protest. "You don't have to worry about a thing, Mr. French. Memphis will be in good hands. *Professional* hands."

"Terrific," Mr. French said. "I'll be leaving first thing in the morning, so she's all yours until next Friday."

"Great," Stevie said. "Thanks for thinking of us." She waved as Mr. French hurried away. Then she turned to face her friends, who were staring at her silently. "I know, I know," she said. "You don't have to say it. Am I crazy? The answer is no."

"The answer is we don't know the first thing about training a Tennessee walking horse," Carole replied.

Stevie shrugged and grinned weakly. "Come on," she said. "We're The Saddle Club. We can figure it out. You seemed to know exactly what Mr. French was talking about just now."

"Only because I've read about it, not because I have any actual experience," Carole said. "I've never even ridden a Tennessee walking horse before."

"Neither had Mr. French before he got Memphis, and he's doing just fine," Stevie pointed out. "And he's not nearly as experienced as we are."

"I just don't know about this, Stevie," Carole said. She realized Lisa hadn't said anything since Mr. French had left. She was staring down at her hands, her brow furrowed as if she were thinking hard. "What do you think, Lisa?" Carole asked.

Lisa looked up. "I think we can do it," she announced.

"What?" Carole was surprised. "A few minutes ago you were worried we couldn't take care of two horses. Now you think we can handle three?"

"Barely," Lisa admitted. "But if we plan it right I think we'll be okay. The way I figure it, I should do most of the work with Honeybee."

"You're actually volunteering to be in charge of that beast?" Carole asked in disbelief. She liked to say she had never met a horse she didn't like, but she had to admit Honeybee came close to changing that.

"Yes. You see, despite all Honeybee's bad behavior, the most important part of that job is going to be keeping Aunt Eugenia happy. And I think I'd probably be the best at that."

"No argument there," Stevie replied.

Carole nodded. "You're definitely the most tactful with adults."

"Meanwhile, Stevie will be in charge of Romeo's training," Lisa went on.

"Because she's the best at dressage," Carole guessed.

"Right," Lisa confirmed. "And that leaves you with Memphis. I know you don't know much about how to train her, but Stevie and I know even less." She shrugged. "What do you think?"

"I guess I can do a little research," Carole said slowly. "I have some books at home that might have a few tips."

"That's the spirit," Stevie said. "See? This is what teamwork is all about."

"True," Carole said. "Although I think next time one of the team members decides to take on more clients, she should discuss it with the rest of the team *first*." She gave Stevie a meaningful look.

But Stevie wasn't paying attention. "Just think of all the

money we'll be making," she said happily. "It's hard to believe that two days ago that bridle and everything seemed totally out of reach. But now we're almost halfway there."

Lisa added the numbers quickly in her head. "Hey, you're right," she said. "Once these horse-sitting jobs are over, maybe we can come up with a way—a *sensible* way, that is—to earn the rest of the money." She sighed. "I can almost feel my gorgeous new chaps right now."

"Well, enjoy it while you can," Carole warned. "Because I have the funniest feeling that all we're going to be feeling for the next week or so is *tired*."

THAT EVENING AFTER helping with the dinner dishes, Carole sat in the living room poring over one of her books. "You know, Tennessee walking horses are really fascinating," she told her father.

"Hmm?" Colonel Hanson replied, looking up from the magazine he was reading. "Why's that, honey?"

"Well, for one thing, their walk is as fast as most horses' trots. And of course it's much smoother. So they're great for endurance riding, as well as lots of other things." Carole sighed and closed the book. "I'll be right back. I've read everything there is in these." She picked up the small stack of books she had brought down from her room and headed upstairs.

She was back a few minutes later with a new stack. "One of

these days you're going to have to start your own equestrian library," her father teased.

Carole smiled. "Very funny," she replied. "But seriously, I'm worried about finding the information I need in any of these books. Most of them just describe the running walk, say that it's mostly natural, that owners can help the horse develop and refine it—but they don't tell you how to go about doing that." She sighed. "I don't want to let Mr. French down." Over dinner she had told her father about Stevie's latest moneymaking plan. He had been a little concerned at how much extra work the girls were taking on until Carole had promised him her school-work wouldn't suffer.

"If I know you girls, you won't let him down," he predicted. "You'll find a way to triumph. You always do."

That made Carole feel a little better. "I hope so," she said.

"Don't just hope," Colonel Hanson said, sounding very much like the lifelong Marine he was. "Do it!"

Carole grinned and saluted. "Yes *sir!*" she replied. She opened one of the new books and got to work. But after a few minutes she closed it and put it aside. "Nothing in this one, either," she said glumly. "I wish I had that set of videos now. It might be more help than these books."

Colonel Hanson looked at her sympathetically, but the phone rang before he could reply. "Just a sec," he said, setting down his magazine and getting up to answer. "Carole, it's for you," he called a moment later.

Carole went to the phone, expecting it to be Stevie or Lisa.

But instead Polly Giacomin was on the other end of the line. She sounded frantic.

"Thank goodness you're there, Carole," she exclaimed. "I already tried Stevie and Lisa and nobody answered at either of their houses."

"What is it, Polly?" Carole asked. "Is it something to do with Romeo?"

"Not exactly," Polly replied. "But you know that my whole family is going out of town, right? That's why I needed you to ride Romeo."

"Right," Carole said.

"Well, that means my little brother Billy will be with us, too. And we just realized he hasn't made any arrangements for Mr. Munch," Polly explained.

"Mr. Munch?" Carole repeated in confusion. "Who's Mr. Munch?"

"That's Billy's pet—oh, wait, hold on a minute," Polly said. Carole heard her shouting to someone downstairs. *"I'm on the phone. . . . Yes, I'm about to ask her. . . . I'll be right there."* Polly's breathless voice returned. "Listen, I've got to be quick," she said. "The thing is, we're leaving first thing tomorrow morning, and Mr. Munch is homeless. So we were wondering if you and your friends would look after him as well as Romeo while we're gone, even though he's not a horse. My parents will pay you for it, of course."

More money meant less time before Carole got those videos. Forgetting about the lecture she'd given Stevie, she said yes immediately.

"Oh, great," Polly said, sounding relieved. "We'll drop him off at Pine Hollow tomorrow morning. I already checked with Mrs. Reg and she said that's all right—she'll watch him until you guys get there after school. Thanks a million, Carole. Really."

"You're welcome," Carole replied. "Just one ques—"

But in the background, she heard someone loudly calling Polly's name. "Hey, I'd better go," Polly said. "I'll see you next Wednesday night, okay? Thanks again." And with that, she hung up.

Carole hung up, too. She thought for a minute. She wasn't too worried about taking on another client. It wouldn't be nearly as much work as the others, since this one wasn't a horse. The only question remaining was what *was* it? Probably a cat or a dog, but which one? The Saddle Club would have to make arrangements to keep Mr. Munch at one of their houses. But Carole didn't want to bring a dog home, since she had a cat. And she knew that Lisa's father was allergic to cats.

She picked up the phone. She knew Polly was busy, but it would only take a second to ask her what sort of creature Mr. Munch was. Although Carole tried several times, the Giacomins' line was always busy.

Finally she shrugged and gave up. It didn't matter. Cat or dog or guinea pig, they could figure it out tomorrow. She returned to her research.

AFTER SCHOOL THE next day Lisa and Carole walked to Pine Hollow together. Carole filled her friend in on the strange conversation with Polly.

"I wonder what it is," Lisa said. "Maybe a fish?"

"With a name like Mr. Munch, it would have to be a barracuda," Carole said with a laugh. "I bet it's a dog. You know Polly's little brother, Billy. He seems like a dog kind of kid to me."

"You're probably right," Lisa said. "Anyway, taking care of a dog or something will seem easy compared to taking care of three horses. Did you have any luck finding out what to do with Memphis?"

"A little," Carole replied. "I had to go through practically every book I own."

"I'm sure you'll do fine," Lisa said. "I just hope I can handle Honeybee."

"Don't worry," Carole said. "We're here to help you with her." She grinned. "It's Aunt Eugenia you'll have to handle on your own."

"Thanks a lot," Lisa said.

"Just kidding," Carole said. "Listen, I'm going to run and check on Memphis first thing. Would you take my stuff to the locker room for me?"

"Sure," Lisa said, taking Carole's schoolbooks from her. "After that I'll probably go see how Honeybee is doing."

"I'll meet you there in a few minutes," Carole said, dashing off.

Lisa carried her things and Carole's to the student locker area and put them away. She glanced at Stevie's cubby. It was in its usual state of disarray, but it didn't look as though anything had been put into it that day. She guessed Stevie hadn't arrived yet.

Lisa headed toward Honeybee's stall. She was only halfway there when she heard Eugenia's strident voice and Deborah's quieter one.

"The girls have to go to school, you know, Aunt Genie," Deborah was saying.

"That's all very well for them," Eugenia replied haughtily. "But what about my darling? They're supposed to be looking after her. How can they do that properly if they don't show up until evening?"

"Hello," Lisa called out politely. She smiled at Eugenia, pretending not to have heard her remark. "How are you doing today, Ms. Eugenia?"

"Very well, my dear," the woman replied rather stiffly. "Can I assume you're here to take care of your duties now?"

"That's right," Lisa said. "I came straight here from school. I thought I'd give Honeybee a good grooming and then let her out in the paddock for an hour or so to stretch her legs."

"That sounds good, doesn't it, Aunt Genie?" Deborah prompted.

"Harrumph. Well, it *sounds* all right, yes," Eugenia said. "But if you don't mind, young lady, I'd like to look Honeybee over after her grooming. Satisfy myself that the job is being done right."

Lisa did her best to maintain her polite smile. "Certainly," she said.

"Do you really think that's necessary, Aunt Genie?" Deborah said. "These girls know what they're doing. You know Max swears by them."

41

"Yes, well, that's hardly a sterling recommendation, now, is it?" Eugenia replied with a frown.

Deborah laughed. "I don't know what I'm going to do with you," she said fondly, giving Eugenia's arm a squeeze. "Come on, now, let's get out of Lisa's way. The least you can do is let her work in peace. We can go up to the house and have a cup of tea. By the time we get back, I'm sure Honeybee will be looking her best." She winked at Lisa and led Eugenia away.

As soon as they disappeared, Lisa let out a sigh of relief. No wonder Max seemed so nervous around Eugenia—but it still seemed strange that he would let himself be intimidated. The stranger thing, though, was how Deborah acted around her. Most of the time Deborah actually seemed to find the bossy old woman amusing. Lisa shook her head. It was all very odd.

Just then Carole appeared from around the corner. "Thank goodness you're here," Lisa said. "Where's Stevie?"

"She hasn't turned up yet," Carole said. "I'm sure she's on her way. What's going on?"

"Aunt Eugenia," Lisa said. At Carole's puzzled look, Lisa quickly explained. "So I need all the help I can get if Honeybee is going to pass inspection when Eugenia gets back from her tea break."

Carole nodded. "No problem. We're all in this together. But first I want to stop by Mrs. Reg's office and make sure Mr. Munch arrived safely."

"And find out what sort of fish, flesh, or fowl he is," Lisa added. "I'm right behind you. I'm dying of curiosity."

The girls hurried toward Mrs. Reg's office off the tack room.

When they arrived, Mrs. Reg was on the phone. She gestured for the girls to sit in the wooden chairs across from her while she finished her conversation.

"Yes, I think that's everything," she was saying. "Now hurry up and get back here. Red already took the adult beginner class out on the trail, but I'm sure he could use your help when they return." She listened for a moment. "Yes, they're both here. They decided to go to the museum tomorrow morning. Listen, I have to go. Carole and Lisa are here. See you soon." She hung up and turned to the girls. "Honestly, that Max! He went to the store to pick up a few things hours ago, and now he calls to see if I want him to stop and get anything else while he's in town." She shook her head. "For the last day or so it seems he's spent more time running errands than he's spent here."

Lisa tried not to smile. She had the funniest feeling she knew why Max was avoiding Pine Hollow as much as possible. He was just trying to stay out of Eugenia's way. And Lisa didn't blame him.

Meanwhile Carole had spotted a large wire cage in the back corner of Mrs. Reg's office. There was a cloth tossed over it so she couldn't see inside.

Mrs. Reg followed her gaze. "Let me guess," she said. "You're here to pick up Mr. Munch."

Carole nodded. "Is that him? Er, we're not sure—That is, Polly didn't tell me—I mean—"

"She means we have no idea what kind of animal Mr. Munch is," Lisa interrupted. "Polly forgot to tell her."

Mrs. Reg laughed. "Oh, really! Well, then you're in for a

surprise." She bent over and pulled the cloth off the cage. Inside sat a three-foot-long green lizard.

Carole gasped. "What on earth is that?"

"It's an iguana," Mrs. Reg said. "They make quite good pets, actually. Max had one as a boy. It was quite an unusual thing then, but nowadays they're fairly common."

"Wow." Lisa stared at Mr. Munch. He looked back at her, blinking lazily. "My mother would really, really hate this guy. She's terrified of all reptiles, great and small." She smiled. "But actually he's kind of cute, isn't he?" She crouched down in front of the cage and stuck her fingers in to scratch the iguana on the head. He closed his eyes, seeming to enjoy the attention.

"He is," Carole agreed. She frowned. "But we may have a problem here. If your mother is scared of reptiles, I guess she wouldn't be too happy about you bringing this one home for the next week, huh?"

"Are you kidding?" Lisa said. "She'd move out. Or rather, she'd make *me* move out. And take Mr. Munch with me." She shook her head. "Sorry. If he was a dog, or maybe a bird, I could talk her into it. But a lizard? No way. Why don't you take him? Snowball isn't likely to bother him. He's too big."

"I think he'd be more likely to bother Snowball than the other way around," Carole said, thinking of her small black cat. "But Snowball's not the problem. My dad is. He hates lizards."

"You're kidding," Lisa said.

Mrs. Reg looked surprised, too. "You mean your father, a big strong Marine, would be afraid of an innocent creature like this?"

44

Carole glanced at Mr. Munch. He did look innocent, but he also looked like a big, green, scaly lizard. "Believe it or not, it's true," she said. "He had a bad experience with lizards once during a training mission in the jungle somewhere. Something to do with his sleeping bag, I think. Now he can't stand them."

"Well, then, Stevie will just have to take him," Lisa said logically. "Her family always has lots of pets around. They won't even notice an extra."

"Uh-uh," Carole said. "Don't tell me you've already forgotten the Great Chameleon Escape? It was only a month or two ago."

Lisa gasped. "Oh, I had forgotten!"

Mrs. Reg looked curiously from one girl to the other. "What happened?"

"Stevie's brother Michael had a chameleon colony in his bedroom," Carole explained. "He was really proud of it, too. He must have had at least twenty of them in there."

"Until the day he forgot to latch the cover after he fed them . . . ," Lisa said.

Mrs. Reg laughed. "Say no more," she said. "I get the picture."

"Yep," Carole said. "They were finding those chameleons for weeks. The day Mrs. Lake found one under her pillow and Mr. Lake found one in his shoe, they announced a ban on all lizards in the house from that day forward."

Lisa glanced at her watch. "We're going to have to come up with something," she said. "Maybe Stevie will have an idea when she gets here. In the meantime we should get started on Honeybee. I want to make sure she's ready for her inspection."

45

"Mrs. Reg, could we possibly leave Mr. Munch here for a little while?" Carole begged. "Just until we figure out what to do with him."

"Well, I really can't have him in my office," Mrs. Reg replied. "The adult beginner class is out on the trail right now, but they're all supposed to stop in later to pick up their new lesson schedules. I wouldn't want anyone fainting on me—you know how funny some people can be about lizards. But I suppose it would be all right to stick him in the empty stall on the end of the row. Nobody's likely to look in there in the next few hours."

"Thanks, Mrs. Reg," Lisa said. She picked up the cage, groaning under its weight. "We'll make sure he isn't there long."

She and Carole stowed the cage in the empty stall and then hurried back to Honeybee. Working together, they managed to have the old mare gleaming in a matter of minutes. It wasn't easy—Honeybee insisted on nipping at every new piece of equipment the girls pulled out of her grooming bucket. Luckily, however, she seemed to have grown tired of nipping at the girls themselves.

When Eugenia returned, even she had to admit that the girls had done a fine job. "Just see that she gets this kind of care every time," she warned. "Not just when you know I'm coming to check up on you."

"Of course," Lisa said politely. "We wouldn't dream of shirking our duties."

Carole was glad Lisa had spoken up, since she was sure her own response to the old woman's rudeness would have been much different. For one thing, she didn't even know what "shirking" meant. But in any case, she was distracted by the sight of Stevie hurrying across the aisle toward the locker room. Stevie glanced down the aisle and caught sight of her friends, but she just gave them a quick wave and kept going.

"Stevie's finally here," Carole whispered to Lisa as Eugenia, with some huffing and puffing, started lifting each of Honeybee's thick hooves to make sure they were clean.

"It's about time," Lisa muttered back. "Since she missed out on all this fun"—she nodded toward Eugenia, who had her back to them—"I figure she owes us one. So I think it should be up to her to figure out a home for our new friend Mr. Munch."

Carole nodded, forcing her face into a smile as Eugenia turned toward them again. "I couldn't agree with you more."

"I THINK STEVIE'S off the hook," Carole told Lisa a few minutes later as the girls led Honeybee toward the back paddock.

"What do you mean?" Lisa asked, yanking the lead rope out from between the mare's teeth. She opened the paddock gate and the mare wandered through it.

"I mean, I figured out the solution to the iguana problem," Carole replied, latching the gate behind Honeybee. "We'll keep him right here."

"At Pine Hollow?" Lisa asked. "But where? I seriously doubt Mrs. Reg is going to want him in her office all week. And he can't stay in that empty stall. He'll be in the way."

"I thought of a better place. Right over there," Carole said, nodding toward a small shed on the far side of the paddock.

"The garden shed?" Lisa asked. The garden shed was where Max kept the equipment he and Red used to care for the stable grounds. It was full of rakes, hoes, grass seed, and all sorts of other things. It was just large enough for all that and the riding mower Red used to mow the lawns and empty fields. Slowly a smile spread across her face. "It's brilliant! It's close enough for us to get to easily—"

"But enough out of the way so nobody else is likely to see him," Carole finished. "We'll just have to warn Red in case he decides to mow the lawn or something."

"It's a great idea," Lisa said. "I just hope Max goes for it. He's been so unpredictable lately. I wonder if he's back from his shopping trip yet."

"Maybe we should ask Mrs. Reg instead," Carole said.

Lisa shrugged. "She's sure to check with him about something like that," she pointed out. "We might as well just ask him ourselves. Or rather," she said, grinning, "*Stevie* might as well ask him herself. She owes us one, remember?"

The girls left Honeybee nibbling at the grass in the paddock and went inside to look for Stevie. They walked by Belle's stall, but Stevie wasn't there. She wasn't with Romeo, either.

"Let's check the tack room," Lisa suggested.

Carole nodded. "I can't wait to see Stevie's face when she meets Mr. Munch," she said.

"Well, I can't wait to see Max's face when Stevie asks him if we can keep Mr. Munch here," Lisa said. She crossed her fingers and headed for the tack room.

As the two girls rounded the corner, they heard angry voices ahead. It was Max and Veronica, and they were facing off in front of the tack room door.

"I can't believe you'd do something so stupid," Max yelled, his hands on his hips.

Veronica pouted. "I tried to tell you," she cried. "You just haven't been around much lately. Besides, I was sure you'd say yes. I mean, who could say no to Winston Haverford-Smythe?"

"I'll tell you who," Max replied grimly. "Me, that's who. There's no way I can take on six extra horses right now. Especially expensive polo ponies."

Carole and Lisa traded quick glances. Now *this* sounded interesting. They both knew that polo ponies usually weren't really ponies at all. A true pony was a horse 14.2 hands or under. A polo pony was simply a quick, strong, agile horse trained to play polo. There were many owners of polo strings in the area around Willow Creek.

"Come on, Max," Veronica whined. "Mr. Haverford-Smythe is a very important man. If you get on his good side, you'll have it made in the social scene around here. Anyway, I already told him you said yes. And he really needs a place for his horses while their stable is being fumigated."

"Then you'll just have to tell him you made a mistake," Max said sternly. "I have no interest in making the social scene, and even less in taking care of half a dozen polo ponies right now."

"But Mr. Haverford-Smythe already gave his grooms the week

off," Veronica wheedled. "And the fumigators are scheduled to come. You have to do it. I told him Pine Hollow was the best full-service stable in the area."

"That's very nice, Veronica, but the answer is still no," Max said, folding his arms across his chest.

"Please, Max? I'll help," Veronica said. "In fact, I'll do most of the work myself."

"Wow," Carole whispered. "She must really be desperate to impress this Haverford-Smythe guy."

Lisa nodded.

"Hey, what's going on?" Stevie said, walking up behind them. "I've been looking everywhere for you guys."

"Shhh," Carole cautioned. "We're just watching the free entertainment. As far as I can tell, Veronica has volunteered Pine Hollow as the temporary home for a string of six polo ponies whose stable is being fumigated and whose grooms are going on vacation. The only problem is, she forgot to mention it to Max beforehand."

Stevie's eyes widened. "Cool," she whispered.

"You haven't even heard the best part," Lisa added. "Veronica just offered to take care of the horses herself."

"Wow. She must really be desperate," Stevie said.

Carole nodded. "That's what I said." But despite the fact that she was enjoying seeing Veronica put in her place, Carole couldn't help feeling a little worried. She hoped this incident wouldn't put Max in such a foul mood that he would say no to their own strange request.

"You'll have to call the man back and tell him to find another stable," Max told Veronica in his best no-nonsense tone. "I might be able to recommend some alternatives."

"Umm," Veronica said, turning her head to listen to something outside.

Max heard it, too. It was the sound of a vehicle—a very large vehicle—moving into the driveway. "What's that?" he muttered. "The grain delivery isn't due until next week."

Veronica looked panicked for a moment. But then, as The Saddle Club watched, her face relaxed and the look of anxiety was replaced by a sly smile. "I think that's your newest tenants arriving, Max," she said sweetly.

"What?" Max said.

"The polo ponies. Oh, did I forget to mention? They're due to arrive today. Right now, by the sound of it." Veronica smirked. "You'd better get out there and greet them. How would it look if you left them standing around in the driveway? After all, I hear this is the best full-service stable in the area."

Max just stared at her for a moment. "You mean the horses you just told me about—they're arriving *now?*" he demanded, his red face turning an interesting shade of deep purple.

Veronica shrugged. "Sorry about that," she said, not sounding sorry at all. "But it looks as though there's not much you can do now except give in and take the boarders. I've heard Mr. Haverford-Smythe has quite a temper. If you turn his horses away at the doorstep, he'll probably see to it that you never get another boarder again as long as you're in business." She paused and examined the perfectly manicured nails on one hand. "Which may not be long," she added softly.

"Veronica, this is not some kind of game!" Max shouted. The Saddle Club had never seen him so angry. "Taking in boarders is a serious business. I can't in good conscience accept horses I don't have the staff to care for, no matter what you or anybody else says. You know Red and I are up to our eyeteeth in work as it is. You'll just have to go out there and tell your friend he has to go elsewhere."

Veronica shrugged and frowned. "Hey, it's your reputation, not mine," she said sullenly.

Max frowned but didn't say anything else. Carole guessed that he was thinking about what Veronica had said. It was true that it wouldn't look good for Max to turn away business at the last minute. He knew and The Saddle Club knew that it was all Veronica's fault that Max was in this mess, but Mr. Haverford-Smythe didn't know that. He would just think Max was disorganized or, worse, dishonest. Carole hated the thought that Pine Hollow's reputation could be damaged by the likes of Veronica diAngelo.

But before she could ponder it further, she felt Stevie push past her. "Hey, Max," Stevie said. "I have the perfect answer to your problem."

Max sighed. "Stevie, please. I don't have time for any of your crazy schemes right now," he said, rubbing his forehead with one hand. "I have to deal with this first."

"But that's exactly what I want to talk to you about," Stevie said. "I think I know a way to make you *and* the polo ponies' owner happy."

"Uh-oh," Lisa whispered to Carole. "You don't think she's actually going to—"

"The answer is let The Saddle Club Horse-Sitting Service take over," Stevie announced happily.

"She just did," Carole said grimly. "This is it. She's finally snapped."

But Stevie and Max didn't hear her. "What do you mean?" Max asked Stevie, looking cautious but hopeful. "You want to take care of the polo ponies while they're here?"

"Yup," Stevie said. "For half your usual boarding fee, of course."

"Of course." Max rubbed his chin thoughtfully.

"If Red will just include the ponies in his morning feeding rounds, we'll do everything else," Stevie continued. "All you have to do is provide the stalls and the supplies."

"Hey, wait a minute, Max," Veronica broke in angrily. "A second ago you refused to even consider letting me help out."

"That's because I know what your version of helping out looks like," Max said sharply. "These horses need real care, Veronica. And I'm sorry to say that I just don't think you're up to the job." He turned back to Stevie. "Do you really think you can do it? Without neglecting your schoolwork or your other chores?"

"I know we can," Stevie said confidently.

"All right," Max said. "You've got yourself a deal. Come on, let's get out there and meet our newest tenants."

"Yes, let's," Stevie agreed, tossing her head as she brushed past Veronica. "Excuse us, Veronica. We've got an important responsibility to take care of. Oh, but I guess you wouldn't know anything about that, would you?" She stuck her nose in the air and sauntered after Max.

As she followed, Lisa felt a sinking sensation in the pit of her stomach. She was already exhausted from rushing over after school, taking care of Honeybee, and figuring out what to do with Mr. Munch. The Saddle Club still had to fit in training sessions for Memphis and Romeo, as well as take care of their own horses, before they left for the day.

Carole was thinking the same thing. Stevie had really gone too far this time. They were having trouble dealing with three extra horses, and one of those was a fat old mare that didn't even have to be ridden. There was no way they could handle six spirited, highly trained polo ponies on top of that, no matter how much Max was willing to pay them. But how could they tell him that now, when he was counting on them? She was pretty sure he had only agreed to Stevie's crazy plan because he didn't realize how much extra work the girls had already taken on. He knew they were taking care of Honeybee, but she suspected he might have forgotten about Romeo and Memphis. That wasn't like him —but then again, Max had been doing a lot of things that weren't like him lately. Carole's stomach growled, and she sighed. It looked as if dinner was going to be awfully late that night.

*   *   *

THE SIGHT OF the polo ponies temporarily took Carole's and Lisa's minds off their troubles. As the younger of the two grooms who had come with the horses led the first one off the van, the girls gasped. The horse was a compact, athletic-looking bay. As Max took the lead rope and led it into the barn, the girls admired the polo pony's strong, quick gait.

"Wow," Stevie said.

"You can say that again," Carole agreed. She hurried forward to take the next horse from the young groom. This one was black with white front stockings that reached almost to his knees. He looked as though he had some Arabian blood in him, and he also looked lively and curious.

The rest of the polo ponies were just as gorgeous. There were three more bays, each glossier and more muscular than the last. The girls took turns leading the horses into the stable and putting them into stalls under Max's direction. Meanwhile Veronica leaned against a fence nearby, watching everything with a disgruntled look on her face.

As the young groom led the last horse, a sleek gray, off the van, Max excused himself and went inside to ask Red to bring down some straw for the visitors' stalls.

"They're pretty great, aren't they?" said the young groom, a slim man in his early twenties, when he noticed Lisa admiring the gray.

"They sure are," she agreed wholeheartedly. "I can't decide which one is my favorite."

The groom laughed. "I can't either," he said. He held out his hand. "By the way, my name's Mick Bonner."

"I'm Lisa Atwood," Lisa replied, shaking his hand. She called over her friends, who had just returned from inside, and introduced them to Mick.

"It must be great to work with such beautiful horses all the time," Carole said, stroking the gray's sleek neck.

"All horses are beautiful," Mick replied, sounding a little like Carole. He grinned. "These just happen to be more expensive than most."

Lisa gulped, her nervousness returning. She hoped Stevie realized what she'd gotten them into.

"Well, they're really wonderful," Carole said. "It'll be an honor to help take care of them."

"Do you work here?" Mick asked.

"Uh, not exactly," Lisa said. "Max is a little shorthanded right now, so he hired us to take care of these horses for him while they're here."

"We're very experienced," Stevie added quickly.

But Mick didn't seem worried. "That's great," he said. "I had a job as an exercise boy at the racetrack when I was about your age." He smiled. "Although it hardly felt like a job. Working with horses doesn't really seem like work somehow, you know?"

"I know exactly what you mean," Carole said, and Stevie and Lisa nodded.

"Hey, what's the holdup here?" demanded the older groom, a lanky man with thin brown hair and a deep suntan. While the others were unloading the horses, he had leaned against the side of the van smoking a cigarette. Now he strolled over to where The Saddle Club and Mick were standing. "We've got to get

57

going. My vacation starts as soon as we get this van back, you know."

"Uh, sorry, Luke," Mick said quietly. "The girls and I were just talking. I'll take Tempest in now."

"Make it snappy," Luke said, lighting another cigarette. "And try not to waste any more time standing around talking to little girls."

Mick cleared his throat. "These girls will be helping take care of the ponies, Luke," he said. "There are a few things we need to tell them before we leave."

Luke raised an eyebrow and looked The Saddle Club up and down. He exhaled a puff of smoke and frowned. "These kids work here?" he said in disbelief. "What kind of operation is this, anyway?"

Max returned just in time to hear the man's last remark. "Is there a problem here?" he asked.

"There might be," Luke replied. "What's this I hear about a bunch of kids taking care of my boss's horses? They're very valuable animals, you know."

"I'm well aware of that fact," Max replied coldly. "And I can assure you, sir, that I would never ask these girls to take on more responsibility than I thought they could handle. They're more than qualified to care for your horses, and I'm confident they'll prove that to your satisfaction, and to your boss's as well. I'll stake my reputation on that."

Luke shrugged, looking a bit taken aback. "Well, I guess that's exactly what you're doing, then," he muttered. "Come on, Bon-

58

ner. Take Tempest in and then let's get out of here. I'll fill in Regnery here on everything he needs to know."

Mick nodded. "Just show me the way," he said to the girls.

"Carole and Lisa, you'd better go help Red with the bedding for the stalls," Max said. The two girls nodded and hurried inside. "Stevie, you can help take Tempest in," he added. "Put him in the empty stall on the end of the aisle near the tack room."

Stevie led Mick and his charge into the stable building, pausing to let the groom soothe Tempest before leading him in. As soon as they were inside, out of sight of Max and Luke, she broke into a grin. The old Max was back! That little speech had been vintage Max Regnery, and it sounded good. Then her grin faded a little. For the first time she stopped to think about how much extra work the six polo ponies would be. Then she shrugged. The next day was Saturday, and they'd just have to spend the entire day at Pine Hollow. Sunday, too. Then there were only a few more days before all the owners came back. They could worry about next week when they had to. In the meantime, Stevie preferred to think about all the money they would be making. She added the figures in her head. Could it be? Yes, she was sure of it. When all their horse-sitting jobs were complete, The Saddle Club would have more than enough money for the things they wanted—including the beautiful new bridle.

"Take that, Veronica," she muttered.

"Excuse me?" Mick said politely. He had been busy murmuring quietly to Tempest. The gray horse had been perfectly calm until he had been asked to enter the strange barn. Now he looked nervous.

"Oh, nothing," she said. "Just talking to myself. Is he okay?"

"Oh, sure," Mick said, giving the horse an affectionate scratch. "He's always like this his first time in a new building. Don't know why. Once he's had a chance to look around and get his bearings, he's fine."

They reached the empty stall. "Here we are," Stevie said. She swung open the door, expecting to see exactly what she'd seen in the other five stalls—the wooden floor swept clean, the walls scrubbed and spotless, and an overturned water bucket near the door, ready for use. She saw all that in this stall, but this time there was something extra as well. A large wire cage sat square in the middle of the stall—and perched atop it, lazy eyes half closed, was a large, green, scaly iguana.

Stevie glanced over her shoulder at Mick and saw his eyes widen. But the groom didn't say a word. He just backed Tempest up a little so the lizard was out of the nervous horse's view and continued talking to him soothingly.

Suddenly the horse's ears flicked backward, and a second later Stevie and Mick heard Luke and Max coming toward them. Luke was complaining to Max about how long it was taking to get the horses settled.

Stevie jumped into the stall and grabbed the iguana. She had no idea whose it was or how it had gotten there, but she could figure that out later. Right now the important thing was to make sure Luke didn't see it. She shoved the sleepy lizard under one arm, grabbed the empty cage, and hurried out of the stall. She managed to duck around the corner and into the tack room just in the nick of time. Quickly shoving the iguana into its cage, she snapped the door shut and then hurried back to the others.

"What on earth is taking so long, Bonner?" Luke snapped as Stevie returned.

"You know how Tempest gets in a new place, Luke," Mick replied mildly. "You've got to take him in slowly." Ignoring the older man, he turned his attention back to the horse and led him into the stall. Tempest went calmly and immediately began snuffling at the walls around him.

Stevie grabbed the water bucket. "I'll go take care of this," she said.

"I think you might want to take care of putting some straw down on the floor before that," Luke said rudely. "I can't believe it wasn't done before we got here."

"The other girls are dealing with that right now," Max said firmly. "And Stevie will be going to help them—*after* she fills the water bucket."

Luke rolled his eyes. "Well," he drawled in a sarcastic tone, "I hope you won't take this the wrong way, but I think I might just stop by tomorrow and make sure the nags have settled in okay. I'm responsible for them, you know, and I'm sure my boss wouldn't want me to leave them somewhere if I wasn't a hundred percent satisfied it was all right."

Max nodded. "Of course, you're more than welcome to stop in to check on your horses anytime," he said stiffly. "Although I can assure you—"

61

"Hey, Luke, didn't you say something about going to a ball game tomorrow?" Mick broke in.

"Oh, yeah," Luke said with a frown. "I almost forgot."

"If you want, I could stop by for you," Mick offered. "I'm not doing anything special tomorrow."

Luke seemed to consider the young man's offer for a second. Then he shook his head. "No, that won't work. I'm head groom. It's my responsibility. I guess it'll just have to wait until Sunday. I've had these tickets for months. There's no way I'm passing up this game—especially not while I'm supposed to be on vacation."

"Sunday it is, then," Max said, heading for the entrance. "Allow me to show you the way out. And don't worry about a thing. Your horses are in good hands here."

"I can see that they are," Mick said politely. But Luke just grunted in reply.

Stevie watched them go, then quickly filled the water bucket and hung it in Tempest's stall. She found Carole and Lisa a few minutes later, hauling bales of straw toward one of the other polo ponies' stalls.

"Um, listen, guys," Stevie said. "Is there anything you've forgotten to tell me today? You know, like you did really well on a quiz, or your parents decided to put in a tennis court, or, oh, I don't know, Pine Hollow is being invaded by giant green lizards . . ."

Lisa gasped and her hand flew to her mouth. "Oh, no! Mr. Munch! I forgot all about him. But where did you . . . ?"

62

"In the gray polo pony's new stall," Stevie said casually. "But I think they'll get along just fine, don't you?"

"Very funny," Carole said. She paused to wipe the sweat from her forehead. Hauling bales was hard work. "Where did you put him?"

"He's in the tack room," Stevie said. "Now would you mind filling me in?"

They told her the whole story, including Carole's plan to keep Mr. Munch in the garden shed. "I guess we'd better get it over with," Carole said. "You're off the hook, Stevie. I'll ask Max. You guys can keep working on getting those polo ponies settled."

"Oh, yeah?" Stevie challenged her. "How come we have to keep doing this backbreaking work while you get the easy part?"

"Do you want to trade?" Carole asked.

Stevie thought for a moment. Did she really want to explain to Max why there was an iguana in his tack room, and then convince him to let them keep it in his garden shed? Suddenly lugging straw and filling water buckets didn't sound so bad after all, and she said so.

When Carole had gone, Lisa turned to Stevie. "Do you realize what you've gotten us into?" she asked.

"Sure," Stevie replied. She grinned and started singing "We're in the Money."

"But, Stevie," Lisa interrupted her, "we're supposed to earn all that money by taking care of *nine* horses. Nine. *And* one iguana. And in the meantime, we're supposed to do our normal chores, go to school—oh yeah, and eat and sleep if we have any spare time. I'm not sure we can do it."

"But it will all be worth it when we have those things we wanted," Stevie said. "Just imagine the look on Veronica's face when Belle has a bridle identical to Danny's." She grinned. "I bet Veronica will throw hers away immediately. Anyway, I don't see what you're so worried about. The Saddle Club can do anything, remember? And this time, what we're doing is heading for easy street."

"Not so fast," Lisa said grimly. "First we have to survive the next five or six days. And I have a feeling *that's* not going to be easy."

"UGH. MY BLISTERS have blisters," Carole mumbled from her position on the Lakes' living room sofa.

"My blisters' blisters have blisters," Lisa countered, not moving from the spot where she had collapsed on the floor in front of the TV. "Stevie, what was that you were saying earlier today about easy street?"

Stevie groaned. "Don't mention streets to me," she said. "That reminds me of walking. And I can't think of anything I'd like to do less right now. Except maybe stand up." She was sprawled in a large, comfortable easy chair. There was a bag of potato chips on the table beside the chair, but Stevie hadn't eaten any. It required too much effort to reach over and get one.

It was Friday night, and the girls were gathered at Stevie's house for a sleepover. Usually their sleepovers involved more talking than sleeping, but it seemed this one might be an exception. The girls had barely managed to stay awake through their late dinner, which Stevie's parents had reheated for them when they arrived. And when Mr. and Mrs. Lake had offered to take them to the movies, The Saddle Club had been too exhausted to accept. They had barely managed to work up the energy to wave good-bye when Stevie's parents and brothers had left the house.

"I can't believe we got everything done today," Carole said.

As her friends thought back on all the work they'd done, they had to agree with her. The girls had worked hard getting the polo ponies' stalls into shape. They'd also removed the traveling bandages and given each horse a quick grooming. After that, Carole and Stevie had held a joint training session for Memphis and Romeo in the outdoor ring. Meanwhile Lisa had headed to the garden shed. Max had okayed the idea of keeping Mr. Munch there, and Carole had moved the iguana's cage in earlier. But when Lisa opened the door, she found the cage empty, its door swinging open. Just when she started to panic, Mr. Munch strolled toward her from behind the riding mower, and she breathed a sigh of relief. *How did you get out?* she wondered. When she read the care instructions pinned to the cage, she got her answer. Billy Giacomin warned in his notes that Mr. Munch liked to escape from his cage whenever he was bored. And he was very good at it. But Lisa wasn't too worried—the garden shed latched from the outside, so even if the iguana broke free he couldn't get out of the shed. Nobody but Max and Red ever went into the garden shed, and both of them knew the iguana was there. She'd put Mr. Munch back in his cage, fed him, and left, latching the shed door carefully behind her. Then she'd stopped by the nearby paddock to pick up Honeybee. She got the old mare settled in for the night, then made the rounds of the polo ponies for one last check. One of the bays, a gelding named Nighthawk, had managed to knock down his water bucket, so she had to replace the wet straw and refill the bucket. By the time she finished, Carole and Lisa had finished their lesson. All three girls worked together to untack and groom Memphis and Romeo. Then Lisa had volunteered to clean their tack while Carole and Stevie walked Belle and Starlight around the schooling ring a few times to stretch their legs. They agreed gratefully, and Lisa got started on her task equally gratefully. At least she could sit down while she was doing it. Finally, after helping with the evening feeding, the girls had headed to Stevie's house for dinner.

"I can't believe we have to go back tomorrow and do it all over again," Lisa said, rolling over onto her stomach and resting her head on her arms.

"Don't worry," Stevie murmured, her eyes drifting shut. "Tomorrow's Saturday. We'll have all day to get everything done. And it'll be worth it. You'll see." With that, she was sound asleep.

THE NEXT MORNING came early for The Saddle Club. By seven o'clock they were at Pine Hollow, stretching and yawning as they got started on the day's work. They began by parting ways to check on all the horses under their care, giving them each a quick grooming and making sure they'd eaten the breakfast Red had given them.

"Now what?" Lisa asked when the girls met up again in the tack room. "It's too early to start exercising the polo ponies, right?"

Carole nodded. "We want to be sure they've digested their breakfasts. Lisa, you should go take care of Honeybee's medication now. And I hate to say it, but I think Stevie and I should probably start mucking out stalls so we don't have them all to do later."

Stevie yawned and grabbed a pitchfork that was leaning against the wall. "Just the way I like to start the day."

A COUPLE OF HOURS later, Carole dismounted from Tempest's back and led him back inside. He had been a dream to ride—responsive and intelligent—but Carole had been too tired and anxious about everything else she had to do to enjoy it as much as she normally would have. After mucking out stalls for an hour, she had ridden one of the other polo ponies for half an hour, then cooled him down, groomed him, and saddled up Tempest. Luckily Stevie, who had just come in from an hour's work with Romeo, volunteered to clean Carole's first set of tack along with her own.

"Thanks for the ride, boy," Carole said, patting Tempest's neck. The horse snorted and nodded his head. He seemed to be in good spirits after his exercise. Carole wished she could say the same thing about herself.

68

*　　*　　*

MEANWHILE LISA WAS unlatching the door to the garden shed. "Time for breakfast, Mr. Munch," she sang out as she entered. "Sorry it's a little late." She saw that the cage was empty. "Oh, no. Not again," she muttered. She looked around and soon spotted Mr. Munch dozing on the vinyl seat of the riding mower. She scooped him up and shoved him back in his cage.

After she fed the iguana from the bag of food Billy had left, she returned to Honeybee's stall. Eugenia and Deborah were spending the morning at a museum, but she wanted to make sure the old horse looked good when her mistress returned. She pulled out a hoof pick and started cleaning Honeybee's feet.

"READY?" STEVIE ASKED Carole later that morning, hurrying over to where Carole had one of the bay polo ponies cross tied in the aisle. She had just finished exercising him and was giving him a good grooming.

Carole looked up, startled. "Ready for what?"

"Horse Wise, silly," Stevie replied, sounding a little impatient. "It starts in about three minutes." Horse Wise was the name of Pine Hollow's Pony Club. Its meetings were held every Saturday.

"Oh, gosh!" Carole gasped. "I completely lost track of time! I haven't tacked up Starlight yet—Max is going to kill me—"

"Relax," Stevie interrupted. "It's an unmounted meeting today."

"Thank goodness," Carole said. "Come on, help me get this guy back in his stall. Then maybe we can both be on time."

*   *   *

THE HORSE WISE meeting gave The Saddle Club a chance to rest their weary bones. When it was over, they hardly remembered what it had been about. Along with the rest of the class, they had to hurry to saddle up their horses for riding class.

"Belle?" Stevie greeted her horse, pretending to be confused. "Is that really you? I'd almost forgotten what you look like."

Belle just snorted in reply. She reached forward to snuffle Stevie's face.

"Okay, I get it," Stevie said, giving her a pat. "You almost forgot what I look like, too. Sorry about that, but it'll all be worth it in the end. You'll see." She smiled, picturing how wonderful Belle would look in her new bridle.

CAROLE WAS GIVING Starlight a final rubdown after class when she heard the scream. It was loud and shrill, and it came from somewhere outside, in the direction of the back paddock. She dropped the rag she was holding into Starlight's grooming bucket and hurried out of the stall. Stevie emerged from Belle's stall at the same time.

"What's going on?" Carole asked.

"Beats me," Stevie replied. "Come on, let's go see."

They raced outside and discovered a small crowd gathered around the garden shed. Several of the students from their own class were there, as well as some of the adult riders who had the lesson after theirs.

"Oh no," Carole said. She suddenly had the funniest feeling she knew what had prompted that scream. "Mr. Munch!"

Sure enough, when the girls pushed their way past the curious onlookers, they saw the big iguana standing in the doorway, staring out at all the people curiously. Nearby, a middle-aged woman was leaning against the paddock fence while another woman fanned her with her hard hat.

"I just needed a rake," the first woman was moaning. "But then I opened the door and that . . . that *monster* was standing there!"

Stevie turned to face the crowd while Carole grabbed Mr. Munch. "That's it, folks," Stevie announced. "Nothing to see here. Show's over. Move along."

Inside the shed, Carole shoved the iguana back into his cage and latched it shut. "You think you're pretty clever, huh?" she told him. "We'll just have to make sure you don't get out again." She fished in her pocket and pulled out a string that she'd picked up off the tack room floor that morning. She wrapped it several times around the cage door, then sat back on her heels to admire her handiwork. "There, that should do it."

STEVIE WAS LUGGING a heavy bag of feed down the aisle when she heard the annoying sound of Veronica's voice.

"Oh, Red!" Veronica called sweetly from outside Danny's stall. "Could you come here for a minute, please?"

Stevie paused long enough to swipe at her sweaty forehead with one arm. She groaned as she remembered, too late, that she'd just been pouring feed and that her arm was covered with little bits of grain. Now her face was covered with it, too. Stevie glanced at Veronica, who looked cool and perfectly attired as

71

always. It didn't seem fair that The Saddle Club should be working so hard when Veronica had just been hanging around all day doing nothing.

"What is it, Veronica?" Red asked, walking over to her.

Veronica smiled at him insincerely. "Oh, thank goodness you're here. You see, I accidentally knocked over Danny's water bucket and spilled it. I need you to refill it for me immediately."

That was all Stevie could take. With a mighty heave she slung the feed bag over her shoulder and stomped away.

"OH, THERE YOU ARE," Eugenia said, cornering Lisa in the tack room, where she had paused just long enough to wolf down a sandwich. "Hmm, having a little snack, are we? It's best not to eat between meals, you know."

Lisa didn't bother to tell her she wasn't really eating between meals. It was almost three o'clock, and Lisa didn't think the old woman would believe this was the first chance Lisa had had to eat lunch. Instead she just nodded.

"Anyway, I've been looking all over for you and your little friends," Eugenia continued. "I have some lovely news."

Lisa was amazed. Was that a smile on the grouchy old woman's face?

"I've decided to have some dear old friends over for tea next Wednesday," Eugenia said. "That's the last day of my visit here, you know. They live in this area, and I haven't seen them in ages."

"How nice," Lisa said politely. She had no idea why Eugenia was telling her this, but she was afraid to ask.

"I'll need you and those other girls to assist me with the party, of course," Eugenia said, as though that were the most natural thing in the world. "For one thing, I'll want to show off my Honeybee. So I thought the easiest thing would be to hold the tea party here, in that shady spot behind the stable under the big apple tree. You girls will need to see that Honeybee looks her very best that day, braids in her mane and all that."

"Oh," Lisa said, relieved. "Of course."

"And naturally you'll be doing the shopping and the preparations for the party itself," Eugenia continued.

Lisa's jaw dropped. "Um, excuse me?" she said. "I, uh, that is, we aren't really experts at that sort of thing."

"No matter," Eugenia said briskly. "You aren't exactly experts at taking care of horses, either, but you seem to be doing adequately with that so far. And of course I'll pay you a bit extra since it wasn't part of our original arrangement. You can pick up the food at the market in town. Max has an account there; you can charge everything to him. Now, we'll want at least three kinds of tea to choose from, some sandwiches—but nothing too heavy. And a good assortment of sweets. . . ."

"Ms. Eugenia," Lisa said, mustering up her most reasonable and sincere tone of voice, "we really appreciate your thinking of us for this, but I'm afraid it's just not possible. We'll be in school on Wednesday, and we have a lot of work to do here as well, so we really just won't be able to manage. As you said, it wasn't part of our original arrangement." She shrugged. "And I know you wouldn't want us to neglect our duties with Honeybee."

"Oh, pish-tosh," Eugenia said, waving aside her objections. "I won't take no for an answer. Now, I've got to go. I must speak to Deborah about arranging transportation for my friends."

Before Lisa could open her mouth again, the old woman was gone.

CAROLE MANAGED TO PUT aside her worries about getting everything done, at least temporarily, while she rode Memphis. She found that the books she had read were right—Memphis had clearly inherited the ability to do the running walk, and all her rider had to do was help her along. Once Carole had adjusted to the long stirrups she was supposed to use, doing so had been a pleasure. The high-stepping walk was indeed as fast as a normal trot, and much easier to sit. Besides that, Memphis was a good-tempered, personable horse. Carole couldn't help enjoying herself, and she vowed to keep track of Memphis's progress even after the week was over.

After forty minutes, she reluctantly dismounted. "Great work, girl," Carole said, patting the pretty chestnut mare on the neck as she walked her slowly around the ring a few more times to make sure she was properly cooled down. "That was a lot more fun than mucking out stalls, I'll tell you that." As she led the horse inside, Stevie suddenly rounded a corner and skidded to a stop in front of her. Luckily Memphis wasn't spooked by Stevie's sudden appearance, but Carole was. She jumped a foot in the air.

"Sorry," Stevie said. "Didn't mean to scare you. But we've got big problems. Emergency Saddle Club meeting—now."

* * *

74

A TEA PARTY?" Carole repeated in stunned disbelief. The Saddle Club was holding their emergency meeting in the quietest spot they could find, the shady hillside overlooking the back paddock. Carole had quickly stowed Memphis in her stall, promising her a full grooming in a few minutes.

Lisa nodded. "She won't take no for an answer," she said bleakly.

"There's no way we can do it," Carole said, shaking her head. "I'm not sure how we're even going to manage all the horses next week when we're in school all day."

"Didn't you tell her we couldn't do it?" Stevie asked.

"I tried," Lisa said. "I even tried to talk to Max about it. But he was so busy figuring out where to get folding chairs for the party and exactly when Red should mow the lawn that he didn't pay any attention to me."

"This is bad," Carole declared.

But Stevie had that thoughtful look on her face again. "Maybe we can pull it off," she said.

Carole and Lisa just stared at her. "Stevie, I think all this hard work is going to your head," Carole said.

"No, just listen," Stevie said. "Lisa, your mother is around after school, right? We'll have her pick us up and drive us to the supermarket. It shouldn't take more than a few minutes to do the shopping. And they've got that huge deli counter there with all the salads and things already made up. We won't have to do any of the preparations ourselves. We can just dump it all into some nice dishes and we're all set."

"But that really doesn't allow us enough time," Lisa pointed out. "By the time we get out of school, finish shopping, get over here and set up . . ."

"Hmm, maybe you're right," Stevie said thoughtfully. "Well, no big deal. We'll just have to do the shopping on Tuesday. I'm sure everything will keep in Max and Deborah's refrigerator overnight."

"But what about all the other stuff we have to do?" Carole asked.

"We'll manage," Stevie said confidently. "After all, Polly comes home Wednesday, so we don't really have to do much with Romeo. And the polo ponies go home Thursday evening— we can exercise them after the tea party and then give them a really thorough grooming Thursday right after school. Same thing with Memphis—Mr. French comes back Friday." She grinned. "And the best part is, right after the party Honeybee and Aunt Genie will be out of our hair—permanently. They're leaving before dinnertime."

"I still don't think we can do it," Carole said flatly.

Lisa sighed. "There's just one problem with that, Carole," she said. "I don't think we have any choice." She glanced down the hill. "Hey, who's that?"

The others looked, too. An elderly man holding a trowel was walking toward the garden shed. Carole recognized him as a member of the adult riding class. He pulled open the door, glanced down at the ground, and then quickly backed away with a shout.

The girls traded glances. "Oh no," they said in one voice. "Mr. Munch!"

*   *   *

VERONICA WAS LOUNGING in the locker room when The Saddle Club finally dragged themselves there after finishing the last of their chores. Luckily Red had taken pity on them and offered to do the evening feeding himself, so they were free to go. The ponies were exercised, Memphis and Romeo had had their day's training, Honeybee was medicated and polished to a shine. The stalls were clean, the tack was gleaming, and everything was in order.

"What are you still doing here?" Stevie snapped. She was in no mood for Veronica right then. Every limb in her body ached, and all she could think about was gobbling down some dinner, taking a hot bath, and climbing into her nice, soft bed. "Are you trying to think of more stupid little things for Red to do?"

Veronica ignored the dig. "What are you girls doing leaving so early?" she asked innocently. "Don't you have to stay and feed all those polo ponies? Or are you letting Max down already?"

"Give us a break, Veronica," Carole said wearily. "Red is going to feed them on his regular rounds tonight. Not that it's any of your business."

"Oh, I see," Veronica sneered. "Couldn't handle it, hmm? I thought as much. I may have to let Mr. Haverford-Smythe know how you've been slacking off." With that, she flounced out of the room.

Lisa sat down heavily on one of the benches and started to pull off her boots. "Boy, she's really something, isn't she?"

"She sure is," Carole agreed. "She and that grumpy groom,

77

Luke, are two of a kind. I feel sorry for those poor horses. If their groom is that bad, just imagine how horrible Mr. Haverford-Smythe himself must be."

"Mick is awfully nice though," Lisa pointed out.

"True. But Carole's right," Stevie said. "If Veronica likes this Hufferford-Smith guy so much, you know he's got to be a jerk."

"Don't forget, the jerk's groom will be here tomorrow to check on his precious ponies," Lisa reminded them.

Carole groaned. "Now *that's* something to look forward to."

"WELL, ALL RIGHT," Luke said grudgingly. "I guess everything's in order here." He nodded toward The Saddle Club. "Good thing, too. I wouldn't want to be late for my barbecue. I'll tell you, this is the life. All play and no work. It's definitely the way to go."

Lisa smiled weakly. Carole rolled her eyes. Stevie just scowled. It was late Sunday morning and Luke had just completed his inspection. The Saddle Club had been working on the polo ponies since arriving that morning, making sure each of them had a little exercise and a good grooming so they would be in top condition when Luke looked them over. The groom had arrived at Pine Hollow half an hour later than he had said he would, but the girls didn't mind. It gave them a little more time to finish mucking out the horses' stalls.

As soon as Luke left, the girls got back to work. They still had plenty to do that day, and they wanted to get it all done as early as possible so they could finalize their plans for Wednesday's tea party. They knew that once Monday came and school started they wouldn't have a second to spare.

Miraculously almost nothing went wrong all day. The only incident occurred when Red accidentally let Mr. Munch out of the shed. The iguana had chewed through the piece of string Stevie had used to tie his cage shut, and when Red was rummaging for a tool, the wily lizard scuttled for the door. Luckily Lisa had just come outside to check on Honeybee, who was in the paddock. She captured the escaping iguana on the doorstep and tucked him back into his cage, closing the door with a paper clip Red found in his pocket.

At dinner that night, Stevie ate ravenously. Working so hard for the past few days had given her quite an appetite. Naturally, her brothers had noticed and started teasing her about it.

"Hey, Chad, did you hear about the world pea shortage?" Alex asked his brother, staring at Stevie.

"No," Chad said, looking up from his plate.

"Well, you will—if Stevie keeps eating this way," Alex said.

Stevie glared at him. "Hey, Alex, guess what your pea brain looks like," she mumbled around a mouthful of half-chewed peas. She started to open her mouth wide to give him a good view of the contents.

"Stevie! Please," scolded Mrs. Lake.

"Sorry, Mom," Stevie said after swallowing. "I guess I'm a little tired."

"Well, I can certainly understand why," Mr. Lake said. "You girls have been working hard these past few days." Stevie had already told her family about The Saddle Club's latest project. Her parents had been impressed by all the work Stevie and her friends were doing, and her brothers had been even more impressed by how much money the girls were making.

Stevie nodded vigorously. "We're exhausted," she said, giving her parents a piteous look. "See? I can barely lift my fork." She let her hand go limp, dropping a forkful of peas and potatoes back onto her plate.

"Poor baby," Mrs. Lake said sympathetically. "It really does sound like you girls have taken on a lot of responsibility."

"We have," Stevie said. "And it's awfully tiring. All I want to do after dinner is fall into bed." She yawned. "*Right* after dinner."

"Hey, no way," protested Michael, Stevie's youngest brother. "It's her turn to clear the table. I did it last night."

"Stevie," Mr. Lake said. "If you're that tired, you can hit the sack early—right after you finish clearing the table."

Stevie frowned. "Couldn't you make one of *them* do it tonight? I'll make it up later in the week, I promise. I've just been working so hard today . . ."

"We understand, Stevie," Mrs. Lake said. "But just because you've taken on more duties at the stable doesn't mean you can forget about the ones you have at home. And that goes double for your schoolwork, by the way. Have you done your homework yet?"

"Um, well . . ." Stevie suddenly remembered something

81

about a one-page English essay she was supposed to write this weekend. And hadn't her math teacher said something about some word problems? "Not exactly all of it, yet."

"Not exactly?" Mrs. Lake repeated.

"Well, not exactly any of it," Stevie replied, stifling a yawn. "I'll do it . . . as soon as I clear the table."

"That's my girl," said Mr. Lake.

"Why should she bother with homework?" Chad said, grinning. "Soon she'll be so rich she won't ever have to go to school again."

"Yeah," Alex put in. "She can buy the whole school if she wants to. Although if I were her, I'd rather buy a boat. Or maybe a motorcycle."

"Or a mansion!" Michael suggested excitedly. "With a pool table and a bowling alley!"

"That's enough, boys," Mrs. Lake said sternly. "I think it's time to change the subject."

The rest of the family started talking about other things, but her brothers' words had set Stevie thinking. She rested her head on one arm and stared down at the remains of her peas. Yes, this weekend had been exhausting, but it would all be worth it, wouldn't it? Soon Belle would have her new bridle. And after this week was over, maybe The Saddle Club would get more horse-sitting clients. Maybe it wouldn't be a good idea to take on so many at once next time, but school would be out soon and the girls would have plenty of free time. If they had even one client per week, they would be rolling in money before the summer was out. Stevie was too tired to figure out exactly how much money, but she knew it would be plenty. Enough to buy practically anything she wanted. She could get a new saddle for Belle to match her new bridle, and maybe a new bicycle for herself . . . or better yet, a moped.

"A moped," Stevie murmured, not realizing until too late that she was speaking aloud.

"What?" Alex asked. "Did you say a moped? What does that have to do with Michael's baseball team?"

"Sorry," Stevie muttered, her face turning red. "I was thinking about something else."

"Apparently," Mr. Lake commented.

Chad grinned. "I know what she was thinking about," he teased. "She was daydreaming about all the things she's going to buy when she's a rich and famous horse-sitter."

"Hey, when you're rich, would you buy me a yacht, Stevie?" Alex asked.

"I could use a new pair of basketball shoes," Chad put in.

"Me too," Michael cried. "And if you're getting a moped, I want one, too."

Stevie opened her mouth to respond, but then she closed it again without saying a word.

"Stevie? Are you okay?" Mrs. Lake asked, looking concerned.

"Sure," Stevie said wearily. "I'm just too tired to fight with these bozos right now."

Mr. and Mrs. Lake traded glances. "Stevie, why don't you go get started on that homework," Mr. Lake suggested. "I'll clear the table tonight."

* * *

83

AT THE SAME TIME, Lisa was sitting at the dinner table with her parents, telling them all about The Saddle Club Horse-Sitting Service. Mr. Atwood had been out of town on a business trip, and Mrs. Atwood had gone out to dinner with friends the evening before, so this was the first time they were hearing exactly how much work Lisa and her friends were doing.

"You mean you three girls are caring for nine horses all by yourselves?" Mrs. Atwood exclaimed, sounding horrified.

"It's not that big a deal, Mom," Lisa said quickly. The last thing she wanted to do was get her mother all worked up. Mrs. Atwood had never really understood why her daughter liked to spend so much time at the stable, and she was always trying to convince her to take up a more ladylike hobby, like needlepoint or violin.

"It certainly sounds like a big deal to me," Mrs. Atwood protested. "I mean, it seems rather odd that we're paying for you to take riding lessons, and yet you end up doing most of the work yourself."

"That's how it works," Lisa explained patiently. "It would cost a lot more than it does if we didn't all pitch in and help out with the chores. Anyway, we're not paying to take care of these horses. Other people are paying us."

"Can't complain about that," Mr. Atwood put in.

Mrs. Atwood frowned at him. "I certainly can," she snapped. "Poor little Lisa is working her fingers to the bone. Darling, why didn't you tell us you needed money? Perhaps we could talk about raising your allowance a little if you're that short of cash."

"It's not just about the money, Mom," Lisa said. "I like doing stable work. So do Carole and Stevie. That's really why we're doing it." She sighed. Explaining things to her parents was always rather tiring, and Lisa was already exhausted. "Like I said, it's not that big a deal."

"Well, if you say so . . . ," Mrs. Atwood said doubtfully.

"She just did, didn't she?" Mr. Atwood said. "Now, why don't you tell us about your dinner last night? How are Gladys and Evelyn?"

Lisa sighed again as her mother began describing her evening. It wasn't that her parents could really do anything about Lisa's difficult week. She just wished they understood.

COLONEL HANSON WAS a little more understanding than the Atwoods, but not terribly sympathetic.

"You took on this responsibility knowingly, Carole," he said, pointing a forkful of chicken at his daughter. "You have to carry through."

"I know that, Dad," Carole said. "I'm not really complaining. Well, maybe I am, but I know we have a job to do and that we have to do it. It's just so much work."

Colonel Hanson nodded. "Does this make you think any differently about working with horses full-time someday?"

"No!" Carole said immediately. "I know that's still for me. But this makes me realize more than ever what a demanding job a stable manager has. I mean, Stevie and Lisa and I have to juggle our time among nine horses, making sure each one is fed, watered, groomed, exercised—all at the right time." She smiled. "Not to mention taking care of one overgrown lizard."

85

Colonel Hanson shuddered. "Don't remind me," he said. "I'm just glad you didn't try to bring that beast into this house."

"Anyway, it takes a lot of planning, and a lot of hard work, and a lot of, um—what's that word you're always using?" Carole asked.

"Discipline! That's exactly what it is," Colonel Hanson said, nodding. He smiled at her proudly. "You've always had that, honey. Runs in the family, you know. But all this work can only improve what nature gave you. That's one of the rules we live by in the military. Hard work builds character."

"Hard work is right," Carole said tentatively. "I didn't realize how hard it would be."

"But you're doing it anyway," Colonel Hanson said. "That's my girl. I'm proud of you, sweetheart. Just like I always am." He began humming a marching tune under his breath.

After that, Carole just ate her dinner in silence.

THE NEXT AFTERNOON after school, Carole and Lisa hurried straight to Pine Hollow and got to work, beginning with the polo ponies. After half an hour, when Stevie still hadn't shown up, they started to get worried.

"It isn't like Stevie to be late on a day like today," Lisa said. "Where do you think she could be?"

"I have no idea," Carole said, hoisting two fresh buckets of water she had just filled. "But we don't have time to stand around wondering about it. She'll get here when she gets here."

"And then we'll kill her?" Lisa guessed.

"No," Carole replied with a grin. "Then we'll make her take care of Mr. Munch."

Another half hour passed before Stevie rushed into the stable,

87

red-faced and breathless. "Sorry," she panted when she found Carole and Lisa in the tack room. "Ran . . . all the way . . . here. Detention. Fell asleep . . . science class. Ms. Cartwright . . . no sense of humor." She collapsed on a trunk and gasped for air. After a moment she regained control of her voice. "Anyway, I really am sorry," she told her friends. "I tried to talk her into giving me a suspended sentence, but no go."

"I was exhausted today, too," Lisa admitted. "I yawned so much during the first two periods that I thought my head was going to crack open."

"Yeah, well, I didn't get to sleep until pretty late," Stevie admitted. "I was up half the night finishing my homework. It's ridiculous. I mean, summer is right around the corner, but my teachers just aren't taking the hint."

"Well, we already decided we might forgive you," Carole said, "if you take care of Mr. Munch today."

"Hey, no problem," Stevie said. "He's the easiest client we have. So where are we on all the others?"

"We're almost done with the polo ponies," Lisa said. "We decided to exercise them on the longe line to save some time, so we only have two more to go. We haven't touched the other three horses yet. We'll do them next."

Stevie nodded. "All right, then," she said. "If you guys can finish up with the polo ponies, I'll take Romeo out and . . ." Her voice trailed off and she grimaced. "Uh-oh," she said quietly. "Don't look now, but I think I hear Aunt Eugenia."

Sure enough, the old woman strode into the tack room a moment later with Max on her heels. "Don't be ridiculous,

Max," she was saying huffily. "I think I know how to tack up my own horse."

"Are you sure you really want to go riding right now, Aunt Eugenia?" Max wheedled. "It's pretty warm out."

"Don't insult me," she replied sharply. "I'm not so old yet that I can't tolerate a little heat."

Meanwhile, the girls were trading panicked looks. If Eugenia went riding now, she would surely notice that The Saddle Club hadn't groomed Honeybee since the night before. And they could just imagine how she would react to that!

"Aunt—er, Ms. Eugenia," Stevie put in, trying to imitate Lisa's tactful talking-to-adults voice. "Maybe you didn't realize it, but Max has some pretty strict rules about trail rides here. One of the most important ones is that riders can never go out on the trail alone. It could be dangerous."

Max nodded vigorously. "Stevie is right, Aunt Eugenia," he said. "If you wait just an hour or two, Deborah will be back from her office. I'm sure she'd love to take you on a lovely trail ride. And it will be much more pleasant then, once the sun has gone down."

Eugenia was silent for a moment, thinking. Then she shook her head. "No, thank you just the same, but I'd rather go now," she said firmly. "And if I'm not to go alone, then one of these girls will have to come with me."

Lisa gulped. She had a feeling she knew which girl it would be.

But Carole stepped forward. "I'd love to go with you, Ms. Eugenia," she volunteered. She had seen the look on Lisa's face.

Since Lisa was the one who had to deal with Eugenia the most, Carole decided the least she could do was spare her friend a trail ride with the crotchety old woman.

Eugenia peered at her. "Very well, then," she said. "Let's be off."

"Um, well, the thing is," Carole stammered, trying to think of an excuse to put off the ride long enough to give Honeybee a quick grooming.

"The thing is," Stevie said quickly, taking over, "I don't think you've had a proper tour of the stable since you arrived."

Eugenia looked suspicious. "I've seen the stable, young lady. I've been here for four and a half days."

Stevie thought fast. "But you haven't seen the polo ponies," she said. "They're really something. Very special."

"Polo ponies?" Eugenia looked interested. "What's so special about them?"

"Oh, all sorts of things," Stevie said, ignoring Max's raised eyebrow. "Just come along with me and I'll tell you all about it." She put a hand on Eugenia's arm and gently led her out of the tack room and around the corner to Tempest's stall. Out of the corner of her eye she saw Carole and Lisa dash in the opposite direction toward Honeybee's stall.

"I really would like to get out on the trail," Eugenia protested. "Couldn't this little tour wait?"

"Oh, it will just take a minute," Stevie assured her. She stopped in front of Tempest's stall, and the curious gray poked his head out over the half door. "See this handsome fellow here? Well, he used to be owned by royalty."

"Really!" Eugenia stared at the horse. "English?"

"No," Stevie said. "Um, Mexican."

"Really," Eugenia said again. "I didn't even know Mexico had a royal family."

"Oh, yes," Stevie assured her. "They're very rich. They have hundreds of polo ponies. They're all gray. Tempest didn't quite match the others, so they had to sell him."

"Very nice," Eugenia said. She turned away. "Now where did that other girl go? I'm ready to ride."

"Not yet!" Stevie said. "Uh, I haven't even shown you the most interesting polo pony. He—um, he was a gift to the president of the United States from a fabulously wealthy Arabian sheikh."

"And he ended up here?" Eugenia said, looking doubtful. But there was a spark of interest in her eyes.

Stevie smiled. "Come with me," she said, taking the old woman's arm again and leading her toward another stall. "I'll tell you all about it."

FIFTEEN MINUTES LATER, when Stevie and Eugenia finally reached Honeybee's stall, Lisa was just slipping on the old mare's bridle. "Here she is, Ms. Eugenia," she said brightly. "All saddled up and ready to go." She carefully checked the girth, then led the horse outside, where Carole was waiting with Memphis.

"I thought I'd kill two birds with one stone," she explained at her friends' glance. She mounted and touched the lucky horseshoe hanging over the door. It was a Pine Hollow tradition. No rider had ever been seriously hurt after touching that horseshoe.

Carole tried to explain the custom to Eugenia. She was pretty sure the old woman was completely confused, but Eugenia reached up and touched the horseshoe without comment.

"That was a close one," Lisa said, as she and Stevie watched the pair ride off across the fields.

Stevie shrugged. "Hey, we pulled it off, didn't we?" she said. "She didn't suspect a thing. And now she can go home and tell all her friends she touched a horse whose sire was once ridden by Elvis!"

STEVIE WAS MUCKING OUT Memphis's stall a few minutes later when she saw Veronica enter Danny's stall across the aisle. Veronica stared icily at Stevie as she walked by, but Stevie ignored her.

"Mucking out stalls again, Stevie?" Veronica said. "Funny, that's all you seem to do these days. Too bad you don't have more of a life."

"Get lost, Veronica," Stevie snapped, shoveling one last forkful of soiled straw into the wheelbarrow standing in the aisle. "I don't have time for your whining today. I have work to do. Or maybe you forgot. Max hired me to help fix *your* stupid mistake, remember?"

"Oh, please," Veronica hissed. "You think you're so great. But you're really just pathetic." She smirked. "I spent *my* Sunday afternoon reading a magazine by the pool. What did *you* do yesterday, Stevie?"

Stevie ignored her. She picked up the wheelbarrow and

steered it down the aisle, narrowly missing Veronica's foot. "Oops, sorry, Veronica," she said sweetly.

When Stevie returned a few minutes later with fresh straw, Veronica was lounging against the wall outside Danny's stall. "Seeing you do all this work gave me a great idea, Stevie," she said. "I don't think Danny likes sleeping on straw. It's too coarse for him. I think wood chips would be much better. They're probably more expensive, but that's okay. I love to buy my horse nice things . . . like that gorgeous new bridle, for instance."

Stevie gritted her teeth and tried to ignore her, but Veronica kept talking. "In fact, I think I'll call Red right now and see if he'll get me some wood chips to try. I'm sure he can clean out this nasty old straw for me right away." She cleared her throat, then sang out, "Oh, Red!"

A few minutes later a harried-looking Red O'Malley appeared. "What do you want, Veronica?" he asked.

"I need you to do something for me," Veronica said. "Danny's bedding needs to be replaced. I want him to try wood chips for a while instead of straw."

Red glanced at his watch. "Look, I really don't have time for this right now, okay? Max disappeared somewhere, and one of his private students just turned up for her lesson. If you're serious about trying wood chips, be my guest. I think there are a couple of bags of cedar shavings in the garden shed. Max was going to use them to lay down a new path, but I'm sure he wouldn't mind if you used some." He hurried away without waiting for a reply.

Veronica scowled. "Why, that lazy, no-good excuse for a groom," she huffed. "I can't believe he just flat-out refused to help me."

"Yeah, hard to believe," Stevie said sarcastically. "After all, he was just sitting around doing nothing while you're here working your fingers to the bone." She snorted. "I can see how concerned you are about Danny. Concerned enough to make someone else take care of him, but not enough to do it yourself. If you even know how."

"Oh yeah?" Veronica shot back. "I know you and your goody-two-shoes friends think I don't know what I'm doing around the stable. I've heard your snotty little comments. But the fact is, I do know what I'm doing just as much as you all do. Just because I'm not always running around trying to prove it doesn't mean I don't. So I think I *will* change Danny's bedding myself. Not because I have to—just because I feel like it." She stomped off down the aisle.

Stevie raised one eyebrow in surprise. She could hardly believe it. Veronica was going to do some actual work? Okay, it wasn't strictly necessary work, since as far as Stevie could tell Danny had no problem with straw at all, but it was work nonetheless.

As Stevie lifted her pitchfork to start shoveling in the clean straw, she heard a loud shriek from somewhere behind the building. She dropped the pitchfork. "Uh-oh," she said aloud. "Mr. Munch!" She grinned and raced off in the direction Veronica had gone. Sure enough, when she arrived at the garden shed, Mr. Munch was perched on the hood of the riding mower, staring at Veronica, who was cowering outside. Seconds later Lisa and Max also arrived on the scene.

"Exactly what is that—thing?" Veronica shrieked. "And what's it doing in the shed?"

"Don't worry," Stevie said, grabbing Mr. Munch and carrying him back to his cage. "He's supposed to be here."

Veronica put her hands on her hips. "I should have known you were behind this, Stevie. It's typical." With that, she stormed away.

Stevie and Lisa tried hard not to laugh. They weren't sure how Max would react. But when they saw him smile, then start to chuckle, they knew they were safe. They burst into laughter.

"Did you see the look on her face?" Lisa exclaimed. "I wish I had my camera with me."

"Me too," Stevie agreed. "That would be one for the photo album. Or maybe the front page of *The Washington Post*. Oh, hey, Max, did you see Red? He was looking for you a few minutes ago."

"No, I just got here," Max said. "I had some, um, errands to do."

Stevie and Lisa traded glances. It sounded as if Max was still trying to avoid Eugenia.

As if on cue, the old woman's distinctive voice floated toward them. Stevie turned and saw Honeybee and Memphis walking in their direction across the back fields.

"I'd better go look for Red," Max said, hurrying away.

Lisa tested the door to Mr. Munch's cage. "He's just going to break out of here again as soon as we leave him," she said.

"Not if I can help it," Stevie said. She glanced around the shed, looking for ideas. "A lock, a lock, my kingdom for a lock," she muttered. Then suddenly she had a brainstorm. She spit out the gum she was chewing and welded it around the latch on his cage. "There! That should hold him," she said. "My mother is always saying that stuff is like concrete when it hardens."

"How are we going to get the door open again ourselves, then?" Lisa asked sensibly.

"We'll worry about that when the time comes," Stevie said casually.

Lisa laughed. "The Stevie Lake philosophy of life."

LISA WAS WAITING at Honeybee's stall to take over when the trail riders returned. She decided Carole had done her part. Lisa could handle the old mare's cool-down and grooming. Luckily Eugenia didn't hang around to watch. She walked up to the house to wait for Deborah to get home.

When Lisa carried Honeybee's tack to the tack room, she found Carole there cleaning Memphis's saddle. Lisa sat down and got to work.

"So how was it?" she asked Carole.

Carole rolled her eyes. "I guess it could have been worse. She hardly insulted Max at all, and she only called me a little girl once or twice. Mostly she just talked about the tea party. From the way she talks you'd think it was the social event of the season."

Stevie walked in. "So this is where the party is," she said when she saw her friends.

"No, the real party is going to be on Wednesday," Carole told her, "when some extremely lovely ladies will be enjoying the lovely warm breezes and nibbling some lovely little sandwiches under the lovely apple tree."

"Uh-oh," Stevie said. "She's really excited about this stupid tea party thing, huh?"

Carole nodded. "All I can say is we'd better make sure it's just as lovely as she's expecting it to be. We're still on for grocery shopping tomorrow, right?"

"Yep," Lisa confirmed. "My mom will pick us all up right after school. We'll have to hurry, though, if we don't want to be late for riding class." She sighed. "Boy, will I be glad when this week is over. Money or no money, it will be nice to have a life again."

And this time, even Stevie couldn't help agreeing.

"DON'T EVEN BOTHER to park," Stevie told Mrs. Atwood on Tuesday afternoon. "We'll be out in five minutes flat."

"All right, dear," Mrs. Atwood said. She pulled the car into the loading lane in front of the supermarket and turned off the engine. "I'll wait right here."

"Thanks, Mom," Lisa said. She, Carole, and Stevie jumped out of the car and rushed inside. The girls were glad to see that the store wasn't crowded.

"All right, where's that list you made?" Carole asked Lisa.

Lisa dug it out of her pocket. "The things Aunt Eugenia specifically asked for I marked with a star, see?"

"If we're going to get everything and still make it to riding lessons on time, we're going to have to split up," Stevie decided, scanning the list. Grabbing it from Lisa's hand, she carefully ripped it into three equal pieces. "Here we go. Now let's get started."

Carole read over her section as her friends hurried off. "Scones," she read. She paused. She had no idea what that was, but it was one of the starred items. "Scones," she said again, glancing around desperately. Maybe she should skip that one and ask Lisa about it when she saw her. The next item on the list was cucumber. Carole nodded happily. She knew what that was.

A few minutes later Stevie was scowling at her list in frustration. She had already found sugar cubes, lemons, and gingersnaps, but the next item had her stumped. She didn't even know how to pronounce it, let alone what it looked like or which aisle it might be in. "Pet—" she muttered, trying to sound it out. "Pet —it—"

"How are you doing, Stevie?" Lisa said, turning into the aisle and hurrying over, pausing just long enough to grab a box of crackers off the shelf. "I'm more than halfway through my list. We might just make it to lessons on time after all."

"Don't be so sure," Stevie said. She pointed to the mystery item on her list. "What on earth is this?"

Lisa looked. "Petit fours," she read. "Oh, yeah, Aunt Eugenia was awfully definite about wanting those. They're like little frosted cakes, about this big." She held her thumb and forefinger about an inch and a half apart. "My mom always gets them for

99

her bridge parties. They sell them here somewhere—maybe in the fancy-foods aisle? Come on, let's check. I have to go there next myself."

"Great," Stevie said. "Let's go."

They didn't even notice Carole as they hurried past the beverage aisle. She was standing in front of a huge wall of tea, dumbfounded. The list specified "loose tea." Carole didn't know what that was, but she would be surprised if they didn't have it here, since they seemed to stock every type of tea ever invented or imagined. She glanced at her watch and gulped. They had already been in the store for much longer than the five minutes Stevie had promised. If they didn't hurry, they would be late for their lesson. They still had to take all this food to the house before tacking up. After all, it wouldn't do to let Eugenia's lemon sorbet melt all over the locker room. Carole closed her eyes and grabbed a few boxes of tea. The ladies would have to make do with what they got.

Carole caught up with her friends in the fancy-foods aisle just in time to hear Lisa talking Stevie out of buying a can of smoked oysters for the party. They had found the petit fours and several other items there, finishing both their lists.

"Are you done?" Stevie asked when she saw Carole.

"Almost," Carole replied. "What's a scone?"

"Come on," Lisa said, turning immediately and heading for the back of the store, where the bakery was. "This way. It's a fancy kind of biscuit-type thing."

Stevie and Carole followed obediently. "How do you know this stuff?" Stevie asked.

"My mother," Lisa said. "She always serves stuff like this when she has people over. She's had a few tea parties in her day herself, you know."

Stevie stopped stock-still in the middle of the aisle and started laughing. The others stopped, too, and stared at her.

"What is it?" Carole asked.

Stevie managed to control herself. "It just struck me as funny all of a sudden," she explained. "Mrs. Atwood probably knows exactly where all this stuff we need is. I bet she could have found it all in ten seconds flat. And we left her sitting outside in the car!"

THE NEXT DAY after school found The Saddle Club back at Pine Hollow once again. If they had felt pressure the day before— they had made it to their riding lesson on time, but just barely— today was even worse. It was the day of the tea party.

"Sorry about the rush, handsome," Carole told Nighthawk as she mucked out the polo pony's stall in record time, leaving him cross tied just outside. "No time for a grooming now, I'm afraid. But I promise, right after the tea party we'll come back and make sure you all get a chance to stretch your legs. Then we'll give you the brushing of your life. And then it's only one more day until you get to go home to your own barn. How will that be?" It sounded good to Carole, especially the part about the horses going home—although she hated to think of the beautiful creatures being under the care of that horrible Luke.

The horse tossed his head from side to side, rolling his eyes at her as she talked. Carole bit her lip. She knew the polo ponies must be restless after being cooped up all day, but there was no time to exercise them right now. They would just have to wait a few more hours.

She finished the job and returned the bay to his stall. "See you soon," she said, giving him a pat. "Be good." As she rushed toward Tempest's stall, she almost collided with Lisa, who came barreling around the corner from the tack room.

"Oh, there you are," Lisa said breathlessly. "I was looking for you. We've got to get up to the house. It's time to start getting the food ready. Aunt Eugenia is waiting for us."

"But we haven't even looked in at all the polo ponies yet," Carole protested. "I just mucked out two of the stalls, but the others must be filthy. And poor Memphis—"

"They'll have to wait," Lisa said. "Don't worry, I checked on all the polo ponies, and their stalls aren't that bad. They can wait a little while. And Memphis is fine. Red said he turned her out in the paddock this afternoon."

"All right," Carole said reluctantly. She didn't like it, but Lisa was right. They would have to let the horses wait while they dealt with the tea party. She sighed. "Since when did this horse-sitting thing turn into Stevie's party-planning idea?" she muttered, following Lisa out of the stable.

"It'll all be over soon," Lisa promised her. "And look on the bright side. At least Stevie's English teacher didn't give her detention when she fell asleep in class today."

Meanwhile, in the kitchen, all was chaos. As soon as Eugenia had looked over the girls' purchases, she had become hysterical. "What is this?" she exclaimed, shoving several boxes of tea in

Stevie's face. "This is not what I specified! I wanted *loose* tea! *Loose* tea! Do you know what that is?"

"Uh, I guess not," Stevie said.

"Aunt Genie, calm down," Deborah scolded. "There's nothing you can do about it now. Anyway, tea is tea. I'm sure your friends won't even notice the difference."

Eugenia tipped her nose into the air. "Perhaps not," she huffed. "But *I* will notice."

"What is loose tea, anyway?" Stevie asked Deborah.

Deborah rolled her eyes. "It's just a different way of making it," she explained. "Instead of putting a tea bag in the pot, you put in loose tea leaves."

"Ugh," Stevie said. "You drink your tea with little things floating in it?"

Deborah laughed. "Well, no. You pour it through a strainer first." She held up a little silver object with holes in the bottom. "It all becomes part of the ceremony of serving the tea."

"Oh, is that all loose tea is?" Stevie said. "Why didn't you say so?" She ripped open the nearest box, pulled out a few tea bags, and looked around for a pair of scissors. Then she cut open the bags and poured the tea leaves out into a bowl. "Voilà! Loose tea!"

Eugenia frowned, but she didn't say anything. Stevie took that to mean she was satisfied with her solution. She was still cutting open tea bags when Carole and Lisa entered.

"Here we are," Lisa announced. "What do you want us to do?"

"Well, first of all, take off those filthy boots," Eugenia said, pointing to Carole's feet. Carole had wiped them on the mat before coming inside, but a few pieces of straw still clung to the sides.

"Aunt Genie, I think we can handle things from here," Deborah said tactfully, taking a pile of plates from the old woman and setting them on the counter. "Why don't you run down and see how Max and Red are getting along? Red must have finished mowing the lawn by now. They'll want you to advise them on where to place the table."

Stevie tried to hide a grin as she snipped the end off another bag. She had the funniest feeling that the last thing Max and Red wanted was to have Eugenia directing them.

"What do you mean, *we?*" Eugenia said. "You shouldn't be helping these girls at all, Deborah. They are getting paid for this, you know."

"I know," Deborah said. "But I don't mind. Besides, they need me here to show them where everything is in the kitchen."

"Hmmph," Eugenia replied. But she allowed Deborah to guide her to the door.

When she was gone, Carole let out a sigh of relief. She grabbed a paper towel and carefully wiped off her boots. "All right, tell me what to do," she said.

Under Deborah's direction, The Saddle Club put together cucumber and butter sandwiches, arranged the scones and other pastries on trays, and set several kettles of water on the stove, ready for boiling.

"Don't forget, once this is done we still have to get Honeybee ready for her grand entrance," Carole reminded her friends.

Lisa nodded. "We'll do it after we carry everything down and arrange the table," she said. She turned to Deborah. "You don't think she'll want to show her to her friends right away, do you?"

"No way," Deborah replied with a smile. "If I know Aunt Genie, she'll want a dramatic entrance. I'm sure she'll wait until they're all settled and a few cups of tea have been had."

"Good," Stevie said. She picked up a plate full of sandwiches in one hand and a pile of napkins in the other. "I guess I'm ready to make the first trip down there."

Deborah picked up a folded tablecloth and tucked it under Stevie's arm. "There. Now you're ready."

While Carole and Deborah finished the last of the preparations in the kitchen, Stevie and Lisa started carrying things to the shady spot behind the stable, where Max and Red had set up a folding table and chairs. As soon as the girls appeared Red made his escape, saying something about a horse needing to be exercised. But when Max tried to sidle away after him, Eugenia called him back sharply.

As Stevie spread the cheerful flowered tablecloth over the table, she heard Eugenia scolding Max. "That horrible big machine is sitting there in plain view," she said irritably. She pointed over to a nearby spot of lawn where the riding mower was standing. "What sort of scenic background is that for a tea party, I ask you?"

Max shrugged. "Sorry, Aunt Eugenia. We just finished the lawn. You wanted it mowed right before the party, remember?"

"I know what I wanted, young man," she snapped. "And I

105

know what I didn't want, too. I didn't want a large ugly vehicle parked where my friends could see it."

"Don't worry," Max said quietly. "I'll go move it right now."

"I'll do it, Max," Stevie offered. Her parents had the same kind of mower, so Stevie knew how to drive it.

"Thanks, Stevie," Max said gratefully. "But don't bother to put it back in the shed. Red needs to use it again later. Just drive it around the side of the barn where it will be out of sight." He hurried off to follow Eugenia's next order.

Stevie was frowning as she climbed aboard the mower and started the engine. She hated seeing Max acting so meek and mild. As much as she sometimes complained about his strictness, the truth was she liked the fact that he always seemed confident and in control. It was different when he got flustered after he first met Deborah. That was understandable—he was falling in love. But now he was acting completely ridiculous around Eugenia, and Stevie had no idea why. She just hoped it would stop when the old lady left. It would be nice to have the real Max back again.

When Stevie finished parking the mower and returned to the party scene, her frown grew deeper. Veronica had turned up from somewhere and was leaning against the apple tree, watching the proceedings. "Having fun, Stevie?" she sang out when she spotted her.

"Get lost," Stevie said. "And do me another favor, okay? Try not to get found."

"Very amusing," Veronica said. "But do you really have time

to stand around being witty right now? It looks like you have a lot to do." She smirked. "Don't mind me. I'll just watch."

Max looked over at that moment and saw the two girls. "Stevie," he called. "Can you come here, please? I need some help clearing these branches away."

Stevie turned and saw that he was picking up twigs from under the tree. She guessed that Eugenia didn't want her guests to have to look at those, either. "Coming, Max."

"Yes, hurry along, Stevie," Veronica said loudly. "Work, work, work."

Max heard her. He stood up and frowned. "Veronica, what are you doing here?" he asked sharply.

"Nothing, Max," Veronica said innocently. "I was just looking for a shady spot to relax in for a few minutes."

"Well, find another one," Max said. "We're busy here. Unless you want to help, make yourself scarce."

Veronica looked annoyed. "It's a free country," she protested. "I'm just standing here."

"And you're certainly free to stand—*somewhere else*," Max said in his best no-nonsense tone.

Veronica didn't protest further. She slunk away, giving Stevie a dirty look as she went.

"LISA, AUNT EUGENIA wants to light some citronella candles to keep the bugs away," Max said. "I think there are some in the garden shed. Would you mind checking?"

"No problem, Max," Lisa replied. It was almost time for Eugenia's friends to arrive. The table was set up, the tea was ready to be brewed, the food looked delicious. In fact, Lisa had to admit that everything looked lovely—just the way Eugenia had wanted it.

She hurried around the corner of the stable to the garden shed. To her surprise, she found Veronica there, hovering just in front of the shed door. "What are you doing here?" Lisa blurted out. Stevie had told her Veronica had left Pine Hollow after Max had yelled at her earlier. Why was she still hanging around?

"Nothing," Veronica replied quickly. "What's it to you, anyway?"

Lisa just shrugged and walked past her. Opening the shed door, she paused to let her eyes adjust to the dim light. Then she scooped up Mr. Munch and stuck him back in his cage. A small twig was lying on the floor nearby, and she jammed it through the latch on his door. It wedged there tightly, aided by the remnants of Stevie's gum. "There, maybe that will hold you, you rascally lizard," she told him. She looked around. Luckily the citronella candles were in plain sight on a shelf. She grabbed them and left. Halfway back to rejoin the others, she paused. Had she latched the shed door? Figuring it was better safe than sorry, she went back to check. The door was shut and latched tightly. Lisa nodded in satisfaction and raced back to the party site.

SOON ALL THAT was left to do was wait for the guests to arrive. That was all that was left for Eugenia to do, that is. The Saddle

108

Club still had to primp and prepare Honeybee for her appearance at the party. They raced to her stall to get started.

"I have an idea," Stevie said. "Since it takes six times as long to groom her when she's always nipping at us, why don't we try doing it outside? That way she can nip at some grass or something instead."

"Great idea," Carole said. "We'll do it in the back paddock. That's out of sight of the party scene, but it's close enough so it'll be easy to bring her over when they're ready for her."

Working fast, the girls hustled Honeybee out to the paddock and got started. Stevie's plan worked perfectly. The old mare was so distracted by all the good things to eat around her that she paid no attention to the girls as they picked out her feet, gave her a brisk grooming, and started braiding her mane and combing out her tail.

They were almost finished when they heard Max's frantic voice calling them from somewhere inside. "I'll go see what he wants," Carole offered.

She hurried inside and found not only Max, but Luke and Mick as well. She gasped. "What are you doing here?" she asked, trying not to sound as nervous as she felt. "I thought the horses weren't supposed to go home until tomorrow."

"They're not," Luke said, giving her a nasty smile. "But I thought it wouldn't be a bad idea to stop by and see how they're doing. You know, a little surprise inspection."

Carole's mind reeled. The polo ponies were certainly not ready for inspection right now. They hadn't been groomed, they

109

were restless due to lack of exercise, and most of their stalls hadn't even been cleaned. She slumped down dejectedly. There was no way out this time. They would have to tell the men the truth. But she didn't want to do it alone. "Wait here for a minute," she said. "I'll go get Stevie and Lisa."

Wʜᴇɴ Cᴀʀᴏʟᴇ ᴛᴏʟᴅ the others the bad news, Lisa looked almost as panicky as Carole felt. But Stevie just looked thoughtful.

"How long would it take you two to get the ponies up to snuff for their inspection?" Stevie asked.

"Too long," Carole said. "Face it, Stevie, Luke's here and ready right now. Even five minutes is too long."

"Not necessarily," Stevie said. "There's nothing we can do about exercising them, but if you guys can get them spiffed up a little—their stalls, too—in the next ten minutes, I might be able to delay them."

Lisa shook her head. "You're crazy, Stevie," she said. "We can't do it in ten minutes."

111

"And there's no way you could stall them that long, anyway," Carole added. "Luke looked pretty determined."

"Make it fifteen, then," Stevie said. She started inside, then paused and turned around. "What are you waiting for? The special Stevie Lake stable tour is pretty fascinating, but there's no time to lose. You'd better get to work." She hurried into the stable.

Carole glanced at Lisa. Lisa shrugged, looking hopeful. "What have we got to lose?" she said.

"You mean besides Max's trust, Pine Hollow's reputation, and our careers as horse-sitters?" Carole said. "Come on. I'll start with Nighthawk. You can take Tempest and go from there." They raced inside.

Stevie strolled up to Max and the two grooms. "There you are, Stevie," Max said, looking a little irritated. "Where's Carole?"

"Oh, she and Lisa had to take care of some things for the tea party," Stevie lied casually. "She sent me here to take care of the inspection."

"Good," Luke said. "Then let's get started."

"I was thinking," Stevie mused. She paused.

"Yes?" Max prompted her.

"Oh, sorry," Stevie said. "I was thinking. Anyway, I was thinking that this might be a perfect time to give our visitors a tour of the stable. You know, show them how Pine Hollow really works."

"Really," Max said, looking amused. Stevie wondered if he

guessed why she was stalling. No matter how distracted he was today by Eugenia's party, Max was sure to have noticed that the polo ponies weren't looking their best at the moment. "Well, I have no problem with that. Carry on, Stevie." With that, he walked away.

"A tour?" Luke said, looking decidedly less than interested in the whole idea. "We really don't have time—"

"Nonsense," Mick interrupted cheerfully. "I'd love to take a look around."

"Forget it, Mick," Luke said. "Let's just check on the horses and get out of here."

"Well, if you say so, Luke," Mick said, looking dubious. "But I'm sure the boss will want to hear all about the place where we took his horses."

Luke paused, seeming to weigh the options. "Maybe you're right," he said finally. "I guess a tour wouldn't be a bad idea. A *short* one."

"Great," said Stevie, trying to hide her relief. Out of the corner of her eye she saw Carole dart across a nearby aisle and duck into one of the stalls. "This way," she said, leading the men in the opposite direction. "We'll start with the student locker room."

"What?" Luke said grumpily. "Who cares about that?"

"It sounds great, Stevie," Mick said. "Very interesting."

Stevie nodded. "Oh, yes. I can't wait to show you each student's cubby."

*   *   *

Ten minutes later Stevie had shown the grooms everything there was to see in the locker room, the bathrooms, the entryway, and Mrs. Reg's office.

"Let's pick up the pace here, all right?" Luke said wearily as Stevie peeked out into the tack room to make sure the coast was clear.

She paid no attention to Luke's comment. Red had just come into the tack room and grabbed a spare grooming bucket. He grinned at Stevie and gave her a thumbs-up sign before darting out again. Stevie's eyes widened. Red must be helping them! Maybe they actually had a chance.

She turned back to the visitors. "Next you'll see our wonderful tack room," she announced. She led them into the cluttered room. "Over here you'll see the saddle I usually use when I ride my horse, Belle," she proclaimed. "And right over there is one of the pitchforks I use to clean out her stall. To the left are some bridles—that one there is snaffle, and right next to it is a double bridle with a curb bit—"

"We know all about that stuff," Luke said, cutting her off. "We do this for a living, you know," He glanced at his watch. "Are we almost finished?"

"Not quite," Stevie said. She patted the top of a trunk. "I haven't even shown you yet where we keep our spare bits."

After another five minutes Stevie's tour had moved on to the outdoor ring. "This is where we hold a lot of our riding classes," she explained. "Max teaches all sorts of people here. There's my class, which is the intermediate class. Then there's a kids' begin-

114

ner class, and one for adults. He also offers private lessons, and sometimes special training sessions and clinics and things."

"Let me guess," Luke put in nastily. "Is this his senior citizen class arriving now?"

Stevie turned and saw that a large blue car had just stopped at the head of the driveway. She had been so busy thinking of new things to tell the grooms that she hadn't even heard it pull in. As she watched, Eugenia and Deborah appeared and hurried forward to greet the three elderly women who emerged.

"Oh, isn't this nice," Stevie said brightly. "The ladies have arrived for their tea party. Let me introduce you." She dragged the reluctant men over and carefully orchestrated the introductions. Deborah and Eugenia seemed a little confused that Stevie was bringing two total strangers over to meet them, but the other ladies were so impressed to hear about the polo ponies that even Eugenia didn't seem to mind.

"All right," Stevie announced to the grooms when the women had disappeared around the side of the building. "Back inside. I just realized I forgot to show you the supply closet where we keep the lightbulbs."

TEN MORE MINUTES passed before Luke finally lost his temper. "That's enough," he exclaimed as Stevie was demonstrating how the faucet on the hose hookup worked. "I couldn't care less which faucet Elvis used when he visited. We've wasted enough time. I want to see the horses. Now!"

"Oh, of course," Stevie said. "First you can see my Belle, then

I can show you Prancer—she's a retired racehorse, you know—
and then—"

"Not those horses, you fool," Luke said through clenched
teeth. "My horses."

"I'd like to take a look at Prancer . . . ," Mick began, but at
the angry look from Luke his voice trailed off. He shrugged at
Stevie helplessly. "Maybe some other time."

Stevie realized that Mick had been trying to help her stall all
along. She gave him a grateful smile. "That's okay," she said. "I
guess we can go see your horses now." She thought fast. During
the tour, she had caught a glimpse of Lisa hurrying away from
Tempest's stall. So he was probably ready for his inspection.
They would start there.

It was touch and go, but they pulled it off. Carole and Lisa
had just finished combing out the last horse's mane and tail
when Stevie and the grooms arrived at the stall. Luckily, Luke
didn't notice a thing. Now that so much time had passed he
seemed more eager to get going than to check the horses. He
just gave them each a cursory glance, not even seeming to notice how restless they were from lack of exercise.

"Well, I guess that's that," he said curtly, closing the door of
the final horse's stall. "Everything looks okay here. We'd better
get going." He gave Stevie a sidelong glance. "Unless you have
any more fascinating rakes or anything to show us, that is."

Stevie smiled angelically. "Nope," she said. "You saw it all."
She stood in the driveway and waved as the two men pulled
away in their truck. Then she raced back inside.

"Are they gone?" Carole asked, intercepting her in the aisle.

"Yup," Stevie confirmed.

"Whew!" Carole exclaimed, collapsing in a heap on the floor. "That was too close for comfort. There's no way we could have done it if Red hadn't helped."

"We really owe him one," Stevie said. "And I think we owe Mick one, too. I seriously doubt Luke would have gone along with the tour idea if he hadn't helped convince him."

Just then Lisa hurried up to them. "Come on," she said. "It's time for Honeybee's grand entrance. Someone needs to get her. Meanwhile, we're also supposed to be pouring tea and stuff. Aunt Eugenia is pretty annoyed that we disappeared like that."

"Oops," Carole said. "I almost forgot. How's the tea party going?"

"Lovely," Lisa replied, rolling her eyes. "It's in full swing. The ladies can't wait to meet Eugenia's darling Honeybee."

"I'll go get Honeybee if you want," Carole offered.

Lisa nodded. "Great," she said. "Come on, Stevie, it's time for our next job of the day—waitressing." The two girls rushed out to the party site while Carole went to get Honeybee. The four old women and Deborah were seated at the table, sipping tea, nibbling on the food, and chattering loudly.

"There you are," Eugenia snapped when she saw the girls. "I hope you realize that Deborah has had to pour the tea since you girls weren't here. Now get over here and make yourselves useful."

They obeyed. Lisa picked up the teapot and started refilling cups, while Stevie picked up the empty cream pitcher and carried it over to the cooler beneath the tree to refill it.

Carole found Stevie there a few seconds later. "Stevie," she said in a strange voice.

Stevie looked up and saw that her friend was pale and trembling. "What's wrong?" she asked immediately.

Carole gulped and glanced furtively at the tea table. "It's Honeybee," she whispered. "She's gone!"

MOMENTS LATER STEVIE'S and Lisa's own eyes confirmed what Carole had told them. They skidded to a stop in front of the paddock. It was empty, and the gate was open and swinging in the breeze.

"How did it happen?" Carole moaned.

"Maybe we didn't latch it right when we left before," Lisa suggested. "We were in an awful hurry."

"I can't believe that fat old thing would even want to escape," Stevie said. "She never showed much interest in anything but eating before."

"Well, you know what they say about the grass on the other side of the fence," Lisa said. "We'd better find her, and quick."

They searched frantically, looking behind the garden shed,

around the front of the stable building, and even inside in the stable aisles, but the mare was nowhere to be seen.

"We've been gone a long time," Carole said worriedly when they reconvened in front of the paddock. "They're going to notice we haven't come back."

"You guys keep looking. I'll go see what I can do back there," Lisa said. "Maybe I can distract them or something." Seeing Stevie's look, she added, "And no, I don't think they'd be interested in a tour of the stable right now." She hurried back to the tea table.

"It's about time, young lady," Eugenia said when she saw her. "Margaret needs some more tea. And where's Honeybee?"

"Um, she'll be here in a minute," Lisa said uncertainly, wishing Stevie were there. She was a much better liar. "Um, Stevie and Carole are, ah, getting her ready."

"I thought you did that earlier," Eugenia said, looking displeased.

"We did," Lisa said quickly. "That is, um—"

"Never mind," Eugenia said brusquely. She stood up. "If these girls can't bring Honeybee to us, we'll just have to go to her. Now where is she?"

"We, uh, put her in the paddock," Lisa said, trying frantically to think of another excuse to stall them.

But it was too late. Eugenia quickly marshaled her friends and led the way, marching around the corner to the paddock. Deborah went with them, not seeming to realize that anything was wrong as she chatted with one of the women about her grandchildren. Lisa followed helplessly. One part of her wanted to

120

break down and confess, but another part resisted. How could she tell Eugenia they'd lost her horse?

Eugenia took in the empty paddock. "Where is she?" she snapped. "I thought you said she was here."

Lisa thought fast. "Um, no, I said we put her here," she said. "Then we decided she might get dirty, so we took her back to her stall."

Looking annoyed, Eugenia spun on her heel and gestured to her friends. "This way," she ordered them. The old ladies followed obediently. Deborah started to do the same, but Lisa grabbed her arm and held her back.

"What is it, Lisa?" Deborah asked.

"We lost her," Lisa hissed.

Deborah looked confused. "What? Lost who?"

"Honeybee," Lisa explained urgently. "We don't know where she is. She's gone. Vanished. Disappeared."

"Uh-oh," Deborah said, glancing ahead at Eugenia's retreating back. "Well, don't worry. She can't have gone far."

Lisa nodded. "Stevie and Carole are looking for her right now."

"Okay," Deborah said. "Come on." She and Lisa hurried after the other women, catching up to them outside Honeybee's stall.

"She's not here either," Eugenia said with a frown. "What's going on here?"

"Oh, I'm sure there's an explanation," Deborah said with a calm smile. "Stevie and Carole must have taken her outside to the party area. Why don't we go back out there now and see?"

"Well, all right," Eugenia said gruffly.

Deborah gave Lisa a wink behind the old woman's back. "Go ahead and help search," she murmured. "I'll try to keep them calm."

"Thanks, Deborah," Lisa said gratefully. As the party goers strolled outside, Lisa stood still, uncertain where to begin looking. They were in real trouble. If they didn't produce the mare within the next few minutes, they really were going to have to confess. And she didn't relish the thought of that at all.

Lisa's thoughts were interrupted, suddenly, by the sound of screaming. It was coming from the direction of the tea party. She gasped. "Oh no," she exclaimed. "Mr. Munch?" She raced outside and saw her worst fears confirmed. Mr. Munch was perched right in the middle of the tea table, chewing thoughtfully on a cucumber sandwich and looking quite content, obviously undisturbed by the shrieking humans surrounding him.

Lisa heard Carole and Stevie gasp as they rushed up behind her. "But how did he get out of the shed?" Carole asked.

"I have no idea," Lisa said. "I closed the door carefully before. I know I did. I even went back and checked it."

Stevie glanced at the women. Deborah and two of the guests were smiling at the sight of the iguana on the tea table. But Eugenia and the other women were quite hysterical and were screaming at the top of their lungs.

"What's going on here?" Max asked breathlessly, rushing onto the scene.

"Um," Stevie began. Even she was at a loss to explain this one.

Luckily Max figured it out. "Stevie, I'd suggest you remove

that creature from the table immediately," he said sternly. But as Stevie hurried forward to comply, she would have sworn she detected a twinkle in his blue eyes.

"Please, Aunt Genie," Deborah was saying. "Please try to calm down. It's only an iguana. See? Stevie's taking it away now."

Max, Carole, and Lisa went forward to try to help. Max laid a hand on Eugenia's arm. "It's all right, Aunt Eugenia," he said. "Everything's under control now."

"First they won't bring my Honeybee out, now this," she moaned. "What next?"

Max turned to Carole and Lisa, looking worried. "I'd suggest you bring her horse out immediately," he whispered. "Maybe that will calm her down."

Carole and Lisa gulped nervously and traded glances. This was it. They couldn't put off their bad news any longer. And after all, Eugenia was already hysterical. How much angrier could she get?

Lisa opened her mouth to confess, but at that moment there was a cheerful shout from around the corner. A second later Stevie appeared, leading Honeybee.

Carole's jaw dropped. Was she seeing things? Or was that really Stevie strolling toward them, jerking her hand from side to side to avoid being nipped by the cantankerous old mare she was leading? For one crazy moment Carole wondered if Stevie had managed to disguise one of the other horses as Honeybee. But no, there was no mistaking that fat rump and ornery disposition.

"Where did you come from?" Eugenia demanded. "I thought you'd gone to take away that nasty reptile."

"I did," Stevie said. "But then I figured I'd stop and pick up Honeybee from the indoor ring." She smiled calmly. "You see, I was on my way out with her when I heard the screams, so I left her there while I came to see what was happening."

Carole and Lisa let out huge sighs of relief. They knew very well that Stevie was lying—the indoor ring was in the opposite direction. But wherever Honeybee had come from, they had never been so glad to see her.

"Oh, she's lovely, Eugenia dear," one of the guests cooed. "Just as you described her."

Eugenia smiled, forgetting all about the girls. She stepped forward and took the lead line from Stevie. "Isn't she, though?" she agreed proudly. The Saddle Club noticed that Honeybee didn't even try to nip her mistress. Then again, that could have been because she was too busy trying to eat the plateful of scones.

The Saddle Club slipped away from the group and huddled under the apple tree. "Where did you find her?" Carole demanded in a whisper.

"The garden shed," Stevie replied. "When I went to put Mr. Munch away, I opened the door and there she was, standing right where the lawnmower usually is."

Lisa gasped. "But how—"

"Veronica, of course," Stevie interrupted. "It had to be her. She must have put her in there to get back at us for taking over the polo ponies. I bet she let Mr. Munch out at the same time."

"Come to think of it, I did see her hanging around near the shed a little earlier," Lisa said. "I can't believe she could be so rotten."

"That's what we always say when she does something horrible," Carole pointed out. "But she always shows us we haven't even begun to see how rotten she can be."

After Honeybee had been properly admired, Deborah offered to take the women inside to wash up after their rather strenuous tea party. The three guests followed willingly, but Eugenia stayed behind. As soon as her friends were out of earshot, she turned to Max. Her face was bright red, and her hands were clenched at her sides.

"I have never been so humiliated in my entire life!" she shrieked at him. "My party is completely ruined, and it's all your fault. Yours and these—these irresponsible children you have helping you." She whirled to face The Saddle Club. "I hire you to do two simple things: help with my party and care for my horse. You destroy my party by letting horrible creatures loose on the table, and you can't even produce my horse when I want her. You've been nothing but trouble to me all week long. I think you're just about the laziest, most impudent children I've ever met. Why, if you were my own I'd take you over my knee—"

"That's enough, Eugenia," Max said suddenly. His voice was low but firm, and Eugenia paused, looking surprised.

She put her hands on her hips. "What do you mean by that?" she demanded.

"This is what I mean," Max began, and from there he went

on to tell her in no uncertain terms. Without being rude or nasty, he told her exactly how obnoxious she'd been all week, and that it had to stop. "You've been running these girls ragged since you arrived," he finished quietly, "and they've been very patient with you. I will not stand here and listen to you insult them. Do you understand?"

"Well, I never!" Eugenia huffed. "I can't believe you're speaking to me this way."

"I had no choice," Max said quietly. "Now, I think you owe the girls an apology."

Eugenia just glared at them all for a moment. Finally, she seemed to relent a little. "Hmmph," she said, not really looking at any of them. "I suppose this little incident is best forgotten. After all, it's hardly your fault that creature turned up."

The Saddle Club decided that was as close to an apology as they were going to get. But more importantly, they were amazed and delighted at Max's speech. He was back!

As Eugenia stomped away toward the house, muttering and grumbling, Carole glanced at Max. He glowered back at her, and for a moment she was afraid he was going to lay into them next. They might not have put Mr. Munch on the tea table, but their behavior hadn't exactly been perfect that day, either. She was sure he knew all about the polo pony incident, and probably about Honeybee's disappearing act as well.

But then Max lowered his gaze to the tea table. Stevie was doing her best to keep Honeybee away from it, but the horse insisted on trying to chew on the tablecloth, and her efforts had knocked everything askew. Several teacups had spilled, and the pile of cucumber sandwiches still showed the imprint of Mr. Munch's footprints. It was a ridiculous scene, and Max finally seemed to realize it. He burst out laughing. After a moment the girls joined in.

A few minutes later, as all four of them walked inside to put Honeybee back in her stall, Max cleared his throat. "I guess you girls are probably wondering what's been going on here lately," he said gruffly. "I haven't quite been myself during Eugenia's visit, have I."

It wasn't really a question, so the girls didn't bother to answer. They just waited.

"The truth is," Max went on, "I've been a wimp and I know it."

Stevie couldn't resist. "You said it, not us, Max," she said with a grin.

Max rolled his eyes. "Very funny. But seriously, I just want to apologize. I hadn't quite realized until today how hard you girls have been working the last few days. I never should have let you take on responsibility for those boarders when you had so much to do." He shook his head. "Especially when school is in session. I hope your duties here haven't interfered with your studies."

"Uh, no, of course not," Stevie said, her face turning pink as she remembered falling asleep in class that day.

"It has been a lot of work," Carole admitted honestly. "But somehow I guess we've managed so far."

Max smiled. "Somehow you have," he said. "And I just want

you to know, Red and I will help you out as much as we can from now on. The polo ponies are leaving tomorrow evening, but how about if Red and I see that they get some exercise tomorrow morning?"

"That would be great," Lisa said with relief. She paused. "Although I think we already owe Red one favor," she added, thinking of the way Red had helped them get the horses ready for inspection.

"That's all right," Max said, chuckling. "I'm sure he's not keeping track."

"But, Max," Stevie said, still curious. "Why did you let Eugenia say all those horrible things to you in the first place?" She hoped he wouldn't be angry with her for asking, but she really wanted to know. "We were beginning to think you'd been taken over by aliens or something."

"Not quite," Max said, looking embarrassed. "I guess you deserve an explanation. But I'm afraid it's nothing as interesting as an alien invasion. Do you remember when Deborah and I went to visit Eugenia after our wedding?"

The girls nodded. "It was a couple of months later, right?" Lisa remembered.

"Right," Max said. "And unfortunately, that had given me just enough time to break her wedding gift to us." He grimaced. "Not that it was such a loss. It was a big, swirly glass bowl of some sort, but I'm sure it was very expensive."

"Did she find out you broke it?" Carole guessed.

Max nodded. "Deborah told her during that visit," he said.

128

"She meant it to be a joke, but Eugenia didn't take it that way. And I've been trying to make up for it ever since."

"Why bother?" Stevie said. "She's such an old grouch. Who cares what she thinks of you?"

Max shrugged. "She's family now, Stevie," he said. "I want all of Deborah's family to like me." By this time they had reached Honeybee's stall. "Why don't you let me take care of her this time," he said.

"Thanks, Max," Carole said, surprised. "Are you sure?"

"Of course," he said, sounding a little irritable—in other words, just like his usual self. "You girls have a lot of work to do before you leave tonight, so you'd better get cracking."

The Saddle Club exchanged grins. It was official. Max was back.

AN HOUR LATER Polly found Stevie in the outdoor ring exercising one of the polo ponies. "I'm back," she called cheerfully. "How did it go?"

"No problem," Stevie told her, riding over the fence. "Romeo missed you, but he's been practicing his trotting half-pass and he's doing great."

"Thanks, Stevie," Polly said. "I'm going in to see him." She rushed away.

Carole saw Polly hurry past as she was emerging from the tack room. She stepped back inside, where Lisa was cleaning tack. "Polly's back," she announced. "Let's go get Mr. Munch."

They carried the cage between them and set it down in front

of Romeo's stall. Polly was inside. She poked her head out. "Oh, was Mr. Munch here the whole time?" she asked. "I hope he wasn't too much trouble."

"No trouble at all," Carole said. "He made lots of new friends."

"Good. Billy can't wait to see him." Polly reached into the pocket of her jeans and pulled out a crumpled check. "Here's the money from my parents," she said, handing it to Lisa. "Thanks again for taking care of these guys." She turned to give Romeo a hug.

Carole and Lisa looked down at the check, then at each other. They smiled. They had been working so hard they'd almost forgotten one very important thing: They were getting paid for it. "You're welcome," they said in one voice.

"IT'S HARD TO BELIEVE our careers as horse-sitters are finally over," Carole commented, tightening Starlight's girth one more time before mounting. It was several days later. The Saddle Club had finally said good-bye to the last of their clients two days earlier when Mr. French had returned. Now they were about to set off on a well-deserved trail ride.

"For now, anyway," Stevie said.

Lisa rolled her eyes. "Don't even think it," she warned. "I'm looking forward to some time off." She was already mounted and waiting on Prancer.

Stevie straightened Belle's new bridle before mounting. "Well, it was all worth it in the end, wasn't it?" she said. "Belle has her bridle, you have your chaps . . ."

"And I love them," Lisa said, glancing down at the chaps she was wearing. As soon as they had finished talking to Mr. French on Friday, the girls had gone to the Saddlery and bought the things they wanted.

"And I have my videos," Carole added. "I watched the first one last night after dinner. It was really good." She grinned. "I would have watched the second one, too, but my dad made me go to bed."

"So I guess it *was* worth it," Lisa said as the girls rode out of the stable yard and headed across the fields at a walk. "Still, it's not a week I'd like to repeat."

Even Stevie couldn't disagree with that. "But you'll have to admit, it would have been a lot easier if it weren't for dear old Aunt Genie," she said.

"Well, *easier* might not be quite the right word," Lisa said. "Less outrageously hard, maybe."

"And anyway, it was Aunt Eugenia who started us off, re-member?" Carole pointed out. "She was our first client."

"True," Stevie said. "Still, I have to say I wouldn't mind if I never saw her again. Or her grumpy old horse, either."

"Me too," Lisa said. "But we probably will. She's Max and Deborah's relative, remember?"

"How could we forget?" Carole said. "I'm just glad Max finally stood up to her. I still don't quite understand why he was acting so weird. It didn't seem to make her like him any better, any-way."

"That's true," Stevie agreed. "He acted like his regular self for the end of her visit, and she didn't change her attitude toward him one bit. She didn't even seem to notice the difference."

"I think Deborah noticed, though. And I think she liked it," Lisa said.

"I'm not surprised," Stevie said. "She doesn't tiptoe around Aunt Eugenia, so why would she want Max to?" She shuddered. "I just can't believe someone as nice as Deborah could put up with that old grump."

Carole shrugged. "She's related to her. She has to."

"Well, I'm just glad *I'm* not related to her," Stevie declared. By now the horses had reached the smooth, wide path leading into the woods. "Come on, enough talking. Let's trot!"

AFTER A LEISURELY ride along the twisting forest trails, The Saddle Club reluctantly turned and headed for home.

"That was fun," Lisa said with a contented sigh as the girls walked their horses slowly across the fields. "It feels good just to relax and have a good time in the saddle for a change."

Carole nodded and leaned forward to pat Starlight on the neck. "I know what you mean. I wouldn't want to be a full-time horse-sitter—not right now, anyway. I still don't think we could have managed at all without the help we got from Red. But you have to admit, it was kind of nice to know we were helping people out as well as making money."

Stevie frowned. "Although you'd hardly know it the way some of our clients—the human ones, I mean—acted. After all the hard work we did for her, Aunt Eugenia didn't even bother to thank us."

"And of course good old Luke barely grunted when he picked up the polo ponies," Lisa added.

"Polly and Mr. French thanked us," Carole pointed out. "And Billy Giacomin called me to thank us for taking care of Mr. Munch."

"Still, it would have been nice if the others had said something," Stevie grumbled. "We did work awfully hard, and they should have acknowledged it."

"Public praise shouldn't matter," Carole said. "What's important is that we did the job we were hired to do and earned the money we were paid."

Stevie brightened a little. "Well, that's true. At least they paid us." She shrugged. "But still . . ."

"I know what you mean, Stevie," Lisa put in. "We were super-responsible and hardworking all week, and hardly anyone seemed to notice. It doesn't really matter, but it doesn't quite seem fair, either."

"You know what really isn't fair?" Carole said. "That Veronica isn't getting punished for what she did."

"You can say that again," Stevie said. She had confronted Veronica the day after the tea party with their suspicions. Veronica hadn't exactly confessed—even she wasn't that stupid—but she hadn't exactly denied anything, either. The Saddle Club was more certain than ever that she had been behind Honeybee's disappearance and Mr. Munch's escape. "You know, I bet she actually planted Mr. Munch on the tea table."

"Do you think so?" Lisa said. "She seemed awfully scared of him. I don't know if she'd pick him up—or even touch him."

"She would if she thought it could get us in trouble," Stevie said with certainty.

They were walking into the stable yard by this time. Carole squinted at a strange car in the driveway. "Who could that be?" she asked. There weren't any lessons scheduled for the rest of the day as far as she knew.

"Maybe it's Aunt Genie, back for more," Stevie guessed.

"Ha ha," Lisa said. The girls dismounted and started to lead their horses inside. Max came to meet them in the doorway.

"Hurry and put your horses away," Max said. "Just make sure they're cooled down and untack them. You can do everything else later. There's someone here to see you."

"Who is it?" Carole asked.

"You'll see," Max said mysteriously. "Just come to the office when you're ready." He gave them a wink, then hurried away.

"I wonder what that's all about," Lisa said.

"Maybe someone else wants to hire us as horse-sitters," Stevie suggested.

The other two groaned. "I hope not!" they said in one voice.

Moments later the horses were comfortable and The Saddle Club was hurrying to Max's office. When they arrived, they found Max talking to Mick Bonner, the younger polo pony groom.

Carole gulped. Was there some problem with the horses? Had they done something wrong? She glanced at her friends and guessed by their worried expressions that they were thinking the same thing.

But Mick soon put their minds to rest. He grinned at them.

"Hi, girls," he said. "I'm glad you're here. I guess I should have called before I came over, but I was so excited I had to rush over and thank you in person."

"Thank us?" Lisa said. "For what?"

"I wanted you to be the first to know—I got a promotion," Mick said. "I'm Mr. Haverford-Smythe's new head groom."

The girls gasped. "That's terrific," Stevie exclaimed. "But what about Luke?"

Mick shrugged. "It turned out my boss had been keeping an eye on Luke for a while," he said. "You may have noticed, he's not exactly the most responsible guy in the world."

"I suspected that," Carole confessed. "He seemed a lot more interested in his vacation than he was in the horses."

"He was," Mick said. "In fact, you might be interested to know that he only pulled that surprise second inspection here because his plans for that day got canceled."

Stevie rolled her eyes. "It figures," she said.

"It was hard working under him," Mick said. "He's careless, and he likes to blame his mistakes on others—usually me. I was afraid I would be the one to get fired. But it turns out that Mr. Haverford-Smythe was on to him. He saw exactly what was happening: Luke was messing up, and I was trying to fix all his mistakes. He was just waiting until he was sure I had enough experience for the job before he fired Luke."

"What finally convinced him?" Carole asked.

Mick laughed. "Believe it or not, it was the lightbulbs," he said.

Carole and Lisa looked confused, but Stevie's eyes widened. "You mean my tour?"

"Yep," Mick confirmed. "After we brought the horses back, Mr. Haverford-Smythe came to see them. He started asking about Pine Hollow, and of course Luke couldn't answer half the questions because he hadn't been paying attention."

"But you could," Lisa guessed, "thanks to Stevie's tour."

"And because I was paying more attention the whole time we were here," Mick admitted. "But it was right after I mentioned where you all keep the spare lightbulbs that Mr. Haverford-Smythe asked to speak to me privately."

"Wow," Carole said. "So now you get to be in charge of all those gorgeous horses yourself."

"Hey, I figured if you three could do it, so could I," Mick teased. "But seriously, I've been waiting for a chance like this. I've been working toward it all my life. And it just goes to show, hard and honest work always pays off in the end."

"I'll second that motion," Max put in, giving the girls a wink.

"Well, I'd better get going," Mick said, standing. "I've got a lot of work to do." He shook Max's hand, then each of the girls'.

"Come on, we'll all walk you out," Max offered. They left the office and headed outside.

"Oh, I almost forgot," Mick said, stopping in front of the stable door. "I'm not the only one who wants to thank you for taking such good care of the ponies. My boss was really impressed when he heard that three girls were doing all the work themselves."

"Really?" Stevie said. Out of the corner of her eye, she noticed that Veronica had just appeared from somewhere and was skulking around nearby. Stevie hoped she'd heard Mick's comment—especially since Stevie suspected Veronica had been the one to give Mr. Haverford-Smythe that information.

"That's not all," Mick continued. "Mr. Haverford-Smythe was so impressed that he wants to meet you. I'm supposed to invite you to the next polo match he and his ponies play in. He wants you to be his special guests at a tailgate picnic lunch."

"Wow!" Carole exclaimed. "That would be fantastic. Tell him thanks, and we'd love to come."

Lisa and Stevie agreed heartily. Stevie snuck a glance at Veronica. Whether or not Veronica had heard Mick before, she had definitely heard him now. Her face turned bright red. Stevie nudged her friends, and they saw her, too.

"Anyway, thanks again," Mick said. "I'll see you soon at the polo grounds." He got in his car and drove away, and Max went back inside. The Saddle Club turned to follow just in time to see Veronica storm away, her face now beet purple. They had never seen her so angry.

And The Saddle Club horse-sitters couldn't help agreeing that *that* was the best payment they could ever ask for.

ABOUT THE AUTHOR

BONNIE BRYANT is the author of many books for young readers, including novelizations of movie hits such as *Teenage Mutant Ninja Turtles* and *Honey, I Blew Up the Kid*, written under her married name, B. B. Hiller.

Ms. Bryant began writing The Saddle Club in 1986. Although she had done some riding before that, she intensified her studies then and found herself learning right along with her characters Stevie, Carole, and Lisa. She claims that they are all much better riders than she is.

Ms. Bryant was born and raised in New York City. She still lives there, in Greenwich Village, with her two sons.

Don't miss Bonnie Bryant's next exciting
Saddle Club adventures . . .

With bonus pages about real gold medal riders!

GOLD MEDAL RIDER #54

The Saddle Club is thrilled to be attending an international riding competition, even if it means they have to serve as humble grooms for Beatrice Benner and her horse, Southwood. Beatrice is the most spoiled rich girl they've ever met, but she is a talented rider. Then an accident threatens to end her career. Stevie, Carole, and Lisa want their friend Kate Devine to take over, but does Kate have what it takes to be a gold medal rider?

With bonus pages about real gold medal horses!

GOLD MEDAL HORSE #55

Southwood is the most glorious horse The Saddle Club girls have ever seen. He has more than athletic talent—he has the heart and soul of a champion. What he doesn't ha_____ the Stevie, Carole, and Lisa t_____ ets one, South_____ ost exciting c_____